the stallion
the rabbit
and the shrew

the stallion

the rabbit

and the shrew

Lisa M. Cummins

For Cristina Albino

Once upon a time there was a stallion.

He wasn't exceptionally large as stallions go, but he was very proud, and his great pride more than made up for his size. His nostrils flared as he tossed his mane this way and that.

"Ho, I will trot wherever I will, and there is no one to stop me," he thought.

And so he did.

Up the side of the mountain and down the other side he went. Then he crossed the spreading green valley, splashing his hooves joyfully in the swirling, ice-cold current of the low, wide creek that cut through the valley like a knife blade through soft butter.

And was he afraid of turning his hoof on a loose stone?

Not at all!

Nothing bad was ever going to happen to him. He *knew* it.

"Ho, there!" shouted the stallion at a rabbit who had stopped munching grass and was now standing up to watch the horse frolicking in the water.

At this shout, the rabbit froze, only a single whisker on the right side of his face twitching. He remained upright, sitting on his hind legs while allowing his forepaws to dangle gently from the wrists, just as he had seen the local squirrels do whenever they were lost in thought. He admired much about the squirrels, especially their intellectual and philosophical prowess.

"Ho, there!" shouted the stallion again. "Look at *me*, will you?"

The stallion jumped so that all his weight fell on his two forelegs. Meanwhile, his back legs made a great kick high in the air behind him.

It was all very impressive.

The rabbit thought, *I'm glad I wasn't standing behind him just now.*

The stallion snorted, tossed his head, and trotted up and out of the water, straight up to the rabbit.

"Were you watching? Did you see me?"

"Oh, yes," said the rabbit loudly and boldly, although inwardly he felt timid standing right beside the stallion, whose muscles rippled like the waves of the sea under a glorious, shining coat.

"Well? What did you think?" urged the stallion.

The rabbit slowly closed his eyes and opened them again.

"I think..." he paused, trying to choose truthful words with care and tact. "I think you should be careful jumping around in the river. You could turn your foot on a stone. You could hurt yourself, and I'd hate to see that happen to you."

"*BAH!*" The stallion tossed his head high and uttered a combined snort, whinny and laugh. "I do *not* hurt myself. That is *preposterous*."

"Well. Well. You don't hurt yourself, you say. Well. That's... er... that's very interesting," muttered the rabbit uncomfortably. He lowered himself back onto all fours and buried his nose in the clover, attempting to resume grazing and avoid further conversation.

"Food any good around here?" asked the stallion.

There was something in the tone of the question that irked the rabbit, but the rabbit lifted his head and answered politely. "I like it. Try some if you like." He spread his right paw to indicate the entire green valley.

"Don't mind if I do," said the stallion, and his great muscular neck swung his head earthward so swiftly alongside the rabbit that the little animal froze again and shrank into a tight, egg-shaped ball against the cool earth, his ears flat laid against his back.

"Ha ha ha ha ha!" laughed the stallion with a hearty guffaw. "What are you so afraid of, little rabbit? I don't eat rabbits, you know." And he laughed again, this time at his own joke.

"I'm not *afraid* of you," muttered the rabbit, now relaxed. "You only startled me."

"Well, you startle pretty easily," chortled the stallion through a mouthful of grass.

"Oh, I guess that's rabbits for you," said the rabbit lightly, now attempting to make a joke at his own expense, for he had become so embarrassed about the whole thing that he wanted more than anything for it all to be over.

"Who's that, Ben? Got yourself a new friend?"

The reedy, high-pitched voice was coming from under a sort of tunnel made by a shock of tall grass which had flopped over. Soon, a body emerged from the tunnel, and it turned out to be a shrew. She was so tiny that she made the rabbit seem as large as a stallion in comparison.

"Oh, hello, Shoshanna," said the rabbit. "I actually, uh... I actually just met this gentleman." He turned to the horse. "I'm sorry... Allow me to introduce myself. I'm Ben, and this is Shoshanna. What is your name?"

"My name?" asked the stallion, again lifting his head high and turning his eyes heavenward. "*My* name is Casanova."

Oh, that is just perfect, thought the rabbit with a small sigh. But aloud he said politely, "Pleased to meet you, Mr. Casanova."

"Pleased to meet you, sir," squeaked Shoshanna.

"Likewise, I'm sure," said Casanova, slowly rolling his eyes down from the clouds and nodding once at each animal in turn. Then he turned his gaze to take in all of the wide and gentle valley. His nostrils quivered as he sniffed at the light breeze. Then he stamped his right forehoof impatiently, creating a reddish gash of wet clay in the green turf.

"I'm bored," Casanova declared. "What is there to *do* around here?"

Shoshanna blinked at Ben, mystified, her mouth slightly ajar. Ben blinked back at Shoshanna. Then both stared up at the stallion.

"Do? What do you mean, *do?*" asked Ben. "We do what we always do. What everyone always does."

"Oh," said Casanova in a tone hovering somewhere between disappointment and condescension.

Now, in that valley there has always been a prevailing culture of courteous hospitality, along with a long-standing custom that every question deserves the best answer one can provide, no matter how silly, vapid, illogical or obnoxious that question may be. Ben and Shoshanna, therefore, exchanged quick glances when they heard the tone of Casanova's "oh." Their glances said many things, but in summary, they said, *This will never do. No, no, no. This won't do. The visitor is always right, after all. We must help this poor horse to find out what there is to do around here, and assist him in doing it, to his complete and utter satisfaction.*

"I'm very sorry," said Ben. "I didn't mean to be rude or to disappoint you by my answer. I have a relatively small brain, you see, so you really shouldn't put too much stock in what I just said. I'll tell you what. There are some folks here in the valley who really know things. I could introduce you to them, and you can pose your question. I'll bet they know the answer."

"Are you thinking of taking him to the squirrels, then?" asked Shoshanna, smiling and nodding as though she already knew the answer was yes. "That's a great idea. Could I come along?"

"Of course. I'd love the company," said Ben with relish.

Ben thought very highly of Shoshanna and considered her a close and reliable friend.

"Squirrels, you say?" said Casanova, his eyes narrowing in skepticism.

"Yes. They're the smartest animals in the whole valley," said Ben, nodding repeatedly. "They can answer just about any question. Yes. Absolutely."

"Huh," said Casanova thoughtfully. "I wouldn't have thought they lived long enough to become very wise."

"Oh, not all squirrels do, you're correct about that," said Ben quickly.

Ben's voice was now strong and confident, as he considered himself to be an expert in squirrel studies, and—as was mentioned earlier—he was quite the squirrel aficionado. Squirrel facts and squirrel history were right in his wheelhouse.

"You see," he added, "some squirrels can live as long as thirty years. Perhaps longer than that. That's the kind we have here in the valley, in fact."

"Thirty years!" Casanova let out his breath in a whoosh that made his lips flutter against each other—*prprprpr!*

"That's right," said Ben proudly, eyes closed, a grin of self-assuredness spreading across his face.

Shoshanna squinted up at the sun and then at the afternoon shadows which were beginning their slow, spreading march under the tall trees that lined the valley. "We'd better get there now if we want to catch old Grunfeld awake."

She turned and led the way to the nearest treeline in her skittering, hoppy run, over and around the hillocks and tufts of grass.

As Ben and Casanova followed at a pleasant pace, Casanova lowered his head to whisper to Ben.

"That... that... *thing...*" he made a motion with his nose toward Shoshanna. "What sort of animal is it?"

"*She*," emphasized Ben in a harsh whisper, "is a shrew."

"Huh," said Casanova. "I heard they were pretty mean."

"Some are. But not Shoshanna. She's as sweet and friendly as they come. Oh... except when she is guarding her young. Or if she's very tired. Or very hungry. Or feels threatened. But you know, I suppose when it comes to that, we *all* get a bit snippy under those circumstances."

"True, that," nodded Casanova.

But Ben noticed that Casanova slowed his pace to permit a bit more distance between himself and the shrew.

Before long, the three had reached the edge of the meadow and were standing under the shade of the tree line.

Shoshanna looked at Ben. Ben cleared his throat and raised his voice to call up into the tree canopy. "Ahem. Ben and Shoshanna seek the wise wisdom of The Honorable Judge Grunfeld, on behalf of our visiting friend, Mr. Casanova!"

Instantly, five tough-looking squirrels, muscular, fit, and in the prime of life, raced down three nearby trees and lined up, company front, ahead of them. These comprised the judge's personal security detail, and they meant business. They studied the horse, the shrew and the rabbit with considerable scrutiny, all the while constantly glancing past them to scan the distant surroundings.

"What is the nature of your query?" asked the toughest looking one.

"Mr. Casanova is new to the area," explained Ben. "He has posed the question, 'What is there to do around here?' We could not provide an answer to his satisfaction, and so Mr. Casanova has agreed to refer the matter to the squirrel forum and to Judge Grunfeld."

The toughest looking squirrel made two sharp signals with his right forepaw to the two youngest squirrels at his side. With a flash of their furry tails, they quickly ascended high into the leafy branches of an ancient oak. Not for the first time, Ben held his breath in awe of their acrobatic speed and agility.

As the horse, rabbit and shrew waited patiently, Ben

explained the reason for the delay.

"Grunfeld is pretty old, so he can't come down the tree by himself anymore," he whispered to Casanova.

"Really? How old is he?" asked the horse.

"Ahh..." Ben scratched his head and began counting on all four paws, but then lost count. He never was very good at counting. "I'm sure he's at least thirty winters old. Maybe a few more than that."

"Wow."

"Yeah, so the squirrels designed this contraption to lower him down and raise him back up. Said they saw it at the humans' farm at the edge of the valley. The humans were using a long yellow viny thing that turned on a round squeaky thing, to lift heavy objects high in the air. The squirrels thought it was a perfect solution to Grunfeld's problem. You'll get to see their contraption pretty soon. It's something else."

"Sounds intriguing," murmured Casanova. He stood taller, and his eyes brightened at the prospect of seeing the invention.

Within a few minutes, something like a basket made of woven vines was being lowered smoothly from the high branches above. A fluffy gray tail could be seen dangling over one side— presumably that of the great Grunfeld. The shrew, the rabbit and the horse approached and stood almost directly under the basket, in order to better watch the process.

As they peered up at a strong limb high above, they could see that the squirrels had chewed away the rough bark of that limb to create smooth rings of exposed wood, around which long, rope-like vines had been wound. Five squirrels were assigned to each viny rope to keep hold of it and to slowly lower the basket down. They kept a good grip on the tree bark with their sharp hind claws, grunting slightly as they gradually let down the vines with their forepaws.

Soon, Grunfeld had been lowered to a respectable yet accessible height above the ground, about a foot above Casanova's eye-level. The judge's seat was, according to tradition, always set to a height just higher than the tallest supplicant—a visible reminder of the solemnity of that venerable court.

Grunfeld was old—covered in whitish gray fur from ears to tail—but he sat up straight and tall in his basket, his keen eyes still intelligent and alert.

"Who seeks the wisdom of Judge Grunfeld?" asked a young squirrel who often served as both court reporter and bailiff. This question was a formality, for the security detail had already relayed all the relevant information. The bailiff's ceremonial question was used to mark the opening of the court for a formal hearing.

"I do, Your Honor," answered Ben, looking only at Grunfeld and taking a tiny step forward. He stretched a paw toward the horse. "I seek an audience with you on behalf of Mr. Casanova, a recent visitor to our parts."

"Welcome to the valley, Mr. Casanova," said Judge Grunfeld in a gravelly but not unkind voice.

"Thank you, sir," said Casanova. He bent his right foreleg and gave a low bow of his head.

Ben glanced at Shoshanna in some surprise, and she returned his look with a small smile of wonderment. This was the first time either had seen Casanova display any level of humility or respect. Ben first wondered if any of it was sincere, then thrust that ungracious thought out of his mind.

Judge Grunfeld turned his shiny dark eyes to Ben. "Are you speaking today on behalf of Mr. Casanova?"

"May we confer for a moment, Your Honor?" asked Ben.

Grunfeld nodded.

Casanova lowered his head to Ben's height.

"Would you like for me to officially speak on your behalf?" whispered Ben in Casanova's ear. "I am familiar with proper squirrel procedure. I'd be happy to help."

"Oh, yes. I'd like that very much. Thank you," whispered Casanova.

Ben turned back to the judge. "Yes, Your Honor, I'll be

speaking on behalf of Mr. Casanova today."

"So noted," said Grunfeld, nodding once at the court reporter, who nodded back and scribbled something down. Then Grunfeld looked back at Ben. "Please state your client's query, Mr. Advocate. The court is prepared to hear it."

"Thank you sir. Mr. Casanova has posed the question, 'What is there to do around here?' to which Ms. Shoshanna here and myself were unable to provide an adequate answer. Rather than mull it over at length on our own—and thus pose undue hardship or delay in regard to rendering Mr. Casanova the appropriate hospitality—we thought it best to refer the question to the squirrels, *id est,* to yourself as their acting legal representative, Your Honor. We hereby defer to this court's decision and agree to accept it as binding."

Grunfeld nodded gravely. "It was indeed wise of you to refer the matter to us. Well done, both of you," he said with just the hint of a smile, at which Shoshanna's eyes misted up with gratitude. "Now. I presume you answered Mr. Casanova's question logically, some such statement as, 'what we all do, what we always do,' *et cetera, et cetera, et cetera?"* He made three small circles in the air with his right forefinger, to punctuate the et ceteras.

"Yes, sir. Exactly! But, how could you have known that?" asked Ben in evident admiration.

Grunfeld chuckled. "Oh, I've been around a few winters, young man. And your answer was a fine answer, a fine answer, insofar as *logic* goes."

The several dozen squirrels who had gathered on the ground and on the tree trunks to watch the proceedings nodded knowingly in agreement.

"But now we must consider *intent,*" continued Grunfeld, leaning forward and resting his chin between his thumb and a crooked forefinger. "We must ask ourselves, what did the horse really *mean* when he posed his question? It would not be unreasonable to posit that the horse actually intended, 'I wish to do something entertaining, exciting, or out-of-the-ordinary.' Would that be a reasonable assumption, Mr. Advocate?"

Ben leaned over to confer with Casanova, who nodded vigorously and whispered, "Yes, yes, that is *exactly* what I meant. The guy's a genius!"

Ben turned back to Grunfeld. "My client states that you have hit it exactly right on the head, sir."

"Very good," said Grunfeld. "Now that we have established the true intent of Mr. Casanova's query, we may proceed to attempt to produce a true and factual response. Here, unfortunately, we run headlong into the age-old philosophical question of what exactly constitutes entertainment, excitement, and so forth. For we all recognize the fact that one animal's ho-hum is another animal's zest. Let us assume for the moment that Mr. Casanova, being a horse, is well familiar with meadows, forest and farmland. As such, those surroundings would be unlikely to contain sources of exhilaration or marked enthusiasm. Very well. If this is assumed to be true, then we may safely answer his question with, 'No, sir, there is nothing 'to do' around here... that is, nothing exciting, entertaining, or out-of-the-ordinary.'"

The squirrels again nodded all around, as did Ben and Shoshanna. But Casanova's nose drooped almost to the ground in transparent disappointment.

"However," continued Grunfeld, noting the horse's reaction, "there *is* one other option. Although I wouldn't advise this under ordinary circumstances."

The crowd hushed and stilled. Casanova lifted his head again, ears twitching forward.

"What might that be, Your Honor?" asked Ben.

"Mr. Casanova *could*," mused Grunfeld, "he *could* go beyond the valley, beyond the farm, and out into... the Badlands of Badness."

An audible gasp rippled through the crowd of squirrels. Each turned to his neighbor, blinking ferociously.

Grunfeld leaned back and spread his paws in a defensive

posture. "As I said, I would strongly advise against it. And so would all of *you*, I'd warrant, if you were in my place." He leaned forward again and glared at all the squirrels in the gallery. "However, we must yield to both logic and thoroughness as we attempt to present all possible answers to Mr. Casanova's query. I would be remiss if I did not mention the Badlands of Badness as a possible resolution to the alleged lack of excitement in this valley—er, um, that is, a *lack* according to Mr. *Casanova's* standpoint."

"The Badlands of Badness? That sounds *awesome,*" breathed Casanova with great relish into Ben's ear.

But Ben was frowning deeply.

Shoshanna was frowning deeply, too.

Ben and Shoshanna had heard the many terrible accounts of the Badlands of Badness, but evidently Casanova had not. If Casanova believed it might be awesome to go there, then clearly he had no clue about how bad the badness could actually be out there.

"If it pleases the court," shouted the voice of a squirrel at the back of a group seated off to the right side of the judge.

"Who is that?" scowled Grunfeld, peering out from under his fuzzy gray eyebrows. "Is that you, Smedley?"

"It is, sir. Approach the bench, Your Honor?"

Grunfeld sighed heavily and rolled his eyes, but motioned Smedley forward nonetheless. Smedley made a flying leap and landed artfully on the side of the basket, making it sway gently. The two whispered vigorously back and forth, waving their forelegs animatedly. At the end of the conversation, Grunfeld made repeated shooing motions with both paws in Smedley's face. Smedley leaped down and returned to his former place among his colleagues.

Grunfeld sighed again, unhappily resigned to whatever it was he had to say.

"It has been brought to my attention by a member of the Possibilities Faction"—here Grunfeld caught the eye of the bailiff with a meaningful look, as if to warn him that 'stuff was about to go down'—"that I have failed to exhaust all possibilities in my response to Mr. Casanova's question. What I failed to include is the possibility that Mr. Casanova, in his search for something to do, might perhaps choose to travel *beyond* the Badlands of Badness, and proceed all the way to the alleged Worselands of Worseness."

A torrent of shouting and cursing erupted from the squirrels on both the left and right sides of the judge's seat. Those on the left hurled insults and accusations at those on the right, and vice versa. Casanova, Ben, and Shoshanna took two full steps backward, mouths agape, eyes darting first to one side and then the other.

Grunfeld rose to his feet in the swaying basket with some difficulty. "ORDER! ORDER IN MY COURT!" he shouted, and the commotion among the squirrels subsided into seething grumbling under the breath.

Grunfeld stiffly resumed his seated position. "Now," he huffed, making a gargantuan effort to restore his blood pressure to normal, "I *realize* that the Worselands of Worseness is a highly controversial subject! *Please* spare yourselves—and *me*—the trouble of re-hashing the two sides of the argument for what feels like the hundredth time in as many years. As befits the solemn duty of this court, *I* shall now summarize the viewpoints of *both* sides, and I shall do so *fairly*. My summary will serve not only to keep our proceedings as speedy and cordial as possible, but to educate Mr. Advocate, and Mr. Casanova, and any others present who may not be *aware* of the controversy."

He glared a warning at Smedley first. Then he turned leftward to glare at a squirrel who appeared to be the leader of the opposing party. Both lowered their eyes, as did all their followers. The entire place fell into complete silence, so that the only sound was the faint twitter of distant birds and the light burble of the creek in the meadow beyond.

Grunfeld turned his attention to Ben, Casanova, and

Shoshanna, and spoke in a gentler tone. "The crux of the controversy surrounding the Worselands of Worseness is this. None of us squirrels has ventured farther than a mile into the Badlands of Badness. What became clear to us beyond all doubt—according to all empirical evidence—is that the badness of the Badlands is *exceptionally* bad. So bad, in fact, that we have always been forced to turn back due to lack of food and water, or exposure to the elements, or danger of predators. We have never successfully explored to the end of the Badlands to see what lies beyond. However, we have received numerous reports from migratory birds who have flown great distances beyond the Badlands. These reports claim that there is a far worse land on the other side. However, the vagaries of the avian tongue, coupled with the foreign culture of these flying creatures who hail from distant lands, make accurate translation into our language difficult if not impossible. Our translations of their reports are full of wildly improbable descriptions: mountains that have mouths that spit fire and smoke high up into the air. Rivers that glow yellow and orange at night and are so hot they will burn you alive. Ragged earth covered in black stone with surfaces that swirl like the currents and eddies of a river." He chuckled helplessly and spread his paws. "You realize, of course, that none of this could *possibly* exist, and yet—" he shook his head and looked down at his paws— "and yet, all the eyewitness accounts *seem* to concur. At least, from whatever our limited translation efforts have been able to gather."

A slight murmuring among the squirrels on the left caused Grunfeld to raise his voice again to drown out their sound. "Now, there are two schools of thought among our honored philosophers on both sides of the aisle," he continued. "One school says that, just because we don't know about a thing, it doesn't mean that it can't exist. Members of this school have adopted the maxim: *'We don't know what we don't know.'*"

The squirrels on the left nodded vigorously. One young squirrel looked as though he was ready to pump a triumphant fist in the air, but an elder squirrel beside him reached out a paw to restrain his foreleg.

"The other school of thought," continued Grunfeld, "holds that a fact cannot be called a *fact* unless it is able to be empirically proven by our own five senses, and therefore one should never speculate at all. This group believes that imaginative speculation is one of society's gravest ills, as it is the source of many a false legend, old wive's tale, and dangerous misconception."

"Hear, hear!" shouted a youth from the right side of the clearing.

"Quiet!" barked Grunfeld. "This is a solemn hearing! Do that again, young man, and I'll hold you in contempt! See if I don't!"

The young squirrel seemed to somehow shrink within his own skin.

"There is a third position, a sort of middle ground," said Grunfeld. "It is the place I most often find myself, in fact. This is a position that acknowledges the validity of both sides, which is flexible enough to apply the high ideals of either side—or both at once—to every situation independently, applying wisdom. I fear, however, that those who hold such 'middle-ground' opinions are in the minority today."

He sighed heavily before continuing. "Therefore, here is my suggestion, Mr. Casanova, and it is only just that: a suggestion. Perhaps you might consider traveling through the Badlands of Badness to see what lies beyond. You could then return and report back to us, in the understandable words of our common mammalian tongue. If others would like to accompany you to serve as yet more eyewitnesses and to aid in the journey, that would be most helpful. This suggested course of action might be beneficial for both you and us squirrels. You would have something interesting and novel to do, and we would perhaps obtain better evidence to study and discuss. This presents a unique opportunity for you, Mr. Casanova. Your evident strength and fortitude can carry you much farther into the Badlands than any of us squirrels have gone before. And I can promise you this: if you do choose to make the journey, no matter what you discover on the far side of the Badlands, your name shall be recorded in perpetuity within our annals as 'Casanova the Explorer'—the brave horse who put his own safety at risk to finally put to rest one of the oldest and most divisive debates in squirrel history."

Casanova heaved a deep breath and stared up at Grunfeld. Then he whispered in Ben's ear.

"Am I allowed to speak directly to the judge?"

Ben turned his face up to Grunfeld. "May my client directly address the court, Your Honor?"

"He may," said Grunfeld.

"I accept!" brayed Casanova. "I accept the challenge. I want to explore the Badlands, pass through, and find out what is on the other side."

He stamped his right forehoof so hard that the earth shook a little and the squirrels nearby twitched.

Grunfeld smiled gently. "Mr. Casanova, I must correct a possible misunderstanding on your part. It is not a *challenge* I have posed; it is merely a *suggestion*. And you do realize that you would be taking this journey completely at your own risk. We squirrels shall not be held liable for any badness that you may experience in the Badlands."

"Oh, yes, sir. I get it. I get that," said Casanova, nodding his huge head vigorously. "It's not *you* who challenges me, sir. It is Adventure herself who challenges me! And a challenge from Lady Adventure, well, sir... that is a challenge that no honorable stallion can ever refuse."

"Ah. Well, then," said Grunfeld, spreading his paws on the edge of the basket and leaning back in satisfaction. "That is a different story. Now, perhaps before you depart, you might benefit from speaking to our scouts who have made several forays into the Badlands. Would you like to speak with them?"

"I certainly would be grateful for any tips they could provide, sir," said Casanova.

"Excellent. Bailiff, please arrange for our scouts to meet with Mr. Casanova immediately following dismissal."

The bailiff nodded.

"Our hearing is now dismissed," announced Grunfeld.

"All rise!" cried the bailiff.

The basket holding Judge Grunfeld was elevated back into the tree canopy. Within minutes, the clearing was empty, with the exception of Casanova, Ben, Shoshanna, and six stout and healthy squirrels—presumably the scouts Grunfeld just mentioned.

Shoshanna whispered to Ben, elbowing him gently in the side. "You don't think Casanova's actually going to *do* this thing, do you? Shouldn't we... you know... try to talk to him? Make sure he really understands what he's up against?"

Ben nodded, and his kindly face took on a stern look as he psyched himself up to address this horse of formidable willpower. He drew Casanova aside from the six squirrels before they had a chance to engage him in conversation.

"Sorry, fellas," said Ben, holding up an apologetic paw to the squirrels. "Need to confer with my client. It'll only be a minute."

The squirrels shrugged and turned to one another instead, engaging in conversation about the weather and such. One leaned nonchalantly against an exposed tree root and picked his teeth with a sharp twig.

"What's up?" asked Casanova somewhat impatiently, his muscles quivering. He glanced eagerly at the six scouts, clearly preferring to be over there with them, discussing the Badlands. Had Casanova been wearing a bit in his mouth, he'd literally be chomping at it.

"Look, uh... Casanova. You haven't had much time to think about this decision. And it's a *big* one. I mean, *think* about it. This is the *Badlands of Badness* we're talking about. I'm not sure if you know what kind of place it is that you're about to enter."

"So?" Casanova spit the word out through his horsey teeth

as though throwing down a gauntlet at Ben.

Ben held up both paws. "Please don't misunderstand me. I'm not suggesting you shy away from the journey. Nor am I suggesting you *take* the journey, either. I'm just asking you to slow down. Take a few days to consider. Take some time to learn about the place, maybe make some solid plans first and—"

"Nonsense!" chortled Casanova. "This is no time for hemming and hawing, friend. This is a time for *action*. Besides, those six scouts can tell me all that I need to know, at least for the present. And the rest? Well, the rest, I must leave to Lady Adventure!"

He tossed his mane and trotted proudly back to the six squirrels, who pushed themselves upright from their various leaning positions as he approached.

Ben remained standing right where he was, mouth ajar, watching Casanova talk with the scouts. At his distance, he could catch only snippets of their conversation—phrases like "tough green plants covered in stabby spikes" and "rattling snakes as big around as a tree" and "huge land crawdads that carry death in their tails." He gave up eavesdropping when they began talking about "endless waves of dry sand that burn your paws." Ben had heard all these descriptions before—since childhood, in fact. But Casanova, rather than becoming more concerned or cautious, seemed only to grow more gleeful with each scout's report.

Lost in a daze and feeling utterly helpless to warn the horse of the impending dangers, Ben never noticed Shoshanna's approach. He jumped nearly a foot straight up in the air when he felt her soft whiskers brush his side.

"Oh! So sorry, so sorry," moaned Shoshanna ruefully, wringing her paws miserably. "I *hate* being startled myself! Sorry about that."

"No problem, my friend," said the shaken Ben. He smiled weakly, laying a gentle paw very lightly on her tiny back. "Not your fault, Shoshanna, dear. I just didn't notice you there. I guess I was stuck in my own head just now." He nodded toward the horse. "As you can see, Casanova has completely disregarded my attempts to warn him about the serious nature of the Badlands, and he doesn't seem to be taking the scouts' reports to heart, either. I fear there is nothing we can do to dissuade him from charging on, willy nilly, straight into the Badlands... and 'caution be damned.'"

"Mmmm. Yes," murmured Shoshanna as she gazed at the horse, who was now braying and prancing in circles around the six squirrels as if demonstrating some kind of offensive or defensive battle strategy. "Yes... I can see that."

She paused, and her eyes narrowed shrewdly. "I wonder, though..."

"What?"

She laughed lightly and flapped a paw. "Oh, it's nothing, really. Just an idea. But, remember how Judge Grunfeld suggested that others might accompany the horse on his journey, as witnesses? I'm thinking that maybe... perhaps *I* might accompany him. If Mr. Casanova will have me."

Ben's eyebrows lifted straight to the top of his head. "You? On a journey like that? Really?"

She grinned back at him. The grin was a mixture: half embarrassed, half challenging. "Yes, me. And why not?"

Ben waved both paws in apology. "Oh, gosh. Please don't be offended. I didn't mean that the way it came out. In fact, if anyone knows what a strong and helpful traveling partner you would make, it's me. It's just that I never figured you for the traveling type." He let out half a sigh and gazed across the valley. "You know, in all these years, I never once considered the thought of you—or anyone else I cared about—ever *leaving* this place. In that respect, I guess I always thought you were more like me, Shoshanna. Sort of a homebody, content to stay close to the meadow in which we were born. Not the adventuresome kind."

She closed her eyes and smiled as a gentle breeze ruffled the fur on her tiny face. She breathed it in deeply, so that her tiny abdomen expanded with the effort.

"Close your eyes, Ben," she said. "Smell that."

Ben did, then opened his eyes just a slit to peek at Shoshanna.

"What do you smell?" she asked, eyes still closed.

Ben closed his eyes again and inhaled. "Cow manure from the farm at the end of the valley."

"Uh-huh. And what else?"

"Daisies and clover. Oo! Fresh carrots in the farmer's garden."

"Yep. And what else?"

"The watery smell of the creek. And... is that... is that *elk* urine?"

"It is. But there's something more. Keep sniffing."

Eyes still closed, Ben concentrated on teasing apart the various odors.

"Wait a minute," he murmured. "What *is* that? I never noticed it before."

"You smell it too? Good! It isn't just me, then. See, I've picked it up on the breeze very faintly every now and then, but I just can't identify it. It's a different thing than anything in the valley, or anything on the farm. It's not the smell of a typical man contraption, nor is it a man path. I just can't place it."

"You're right!" said Ben. "It's completely new!"

To his astonishment, he recognized an odd excitement rising in his chest. Not a fearful excitement, but a pleasurable one. It wasn't a familiar feeling for him.

"The one thing I do know about that smell," said Shoshanna, finally opening her eyes, "is that it always comes from the direction of the Badlands. Now. I'm going to ask you to answer truthfully. Wouldn't you just love to find out what makes that scent?"

Ben grinned at Shoshanna and let out a small bark of surprised laughter. "You know what? I would!"

At that moment, Casanova came cantering up to the two. The

six squirrels had vanished, now high up in their trees to spend the night in safety. For the sky had become dusky, and the darkness under the shadow of the tree canopy had reached that treacherous level of gloom which is able to disguise who-knows-what sort of predators. Hundreds of mosquitoes had begun buzzing around in their soft, feathery clouds, and the same number of crickets and frogs were singing at top volume in their nightly performance.

"Let's head out to the open field," suggested Casanova. "At least it's lighter out there. That forest is beginning to creep me out." The skin behind Casanova's shoulders twitched uneasily as he glanced at the trees.

"Agreed," said Ben, who cringed involuntarily at the distant hoot of an owl. "And it's way past time for me to be getting back to my hole, anyway."

"Me too," said Shoshanna with a weary expression.

The three made their way back to the place beside the creek where the stallion had first made his splashy appearance in the valley.

"When do you plan to depart for the Badlands of Badness?" Ben asked Casanova.

"Tomorrow. First light," stated Casanova with the force and certainty of a five-star general issuing battle commands.

"If I may be so bold," ventured Ben, "I would like to offer my services as trail companion on your journey."

"And so would I," added Shoshanna.

Casanova focused his huge round eyes on each small animal in turn, appeared to weigh their offer for a few seconds, then shrugged.

"The more, the merrier!" he said lightly. "We can meet here, right beside this big rock, tomorrow morning. First light."

"First light," repeated Ben and Shoshanna in unison, nodding.

And Casanova turned and galloped away.

The next morning at the earliest gray hint of dawn, Ben

made his way to the big rock. He saw no sign of the horse, so he began licking the dew off his fur to pass the time. Soon he heard a slight scuffling sound and Shoshanna appeared.

"Wow. Wet morning," she said, shaking her paws so that the dew flew off in tiny droplets.

"Ain't it always," agreed Ben amiably.

Casanova's heavy gait could be felt through the earth before it could be heard, even by the keen ears of Ben and Shoshanna, so they were standing on their hind legs searching for him in the foggy gloom long before he arrived in that part of the meadow.

"Mornin', folks," said Casanova pleasantly when he found the two. "Oof! Almost stepped right on you before I saw you! Sorry 'bout that."

"Naw, we would have gotten out of the way," said Ben, flapping a paw. "We're both pretty quick."

"That you are," said Casanova. "I have always envied you smaller animals for your agility. And I often dream about how great it would be to have paws instead of hooves, even if just for a short while. Just to be able to pick up an object without having to use my mouth."

Ben's eyebrows lifted. It hadn't occurred to him that an animal as magnificent as a stallion could envy another animal. He had never even considered the special talents that his and Shoshanna's bodies afforded them. He chuckled to himself. Here he was, already learning new things, and he hadn't yet taken the first step of the journey.

"Are we ready?" asked Shoshanna.

"Ready!" said the horse and the rabbit.

They turned in the direction of the farm at the bottom of the valley. Beyond that farm, they all three knew, lay the Badlands of Badness.

As they approached the farm, they began to change course so as to give it a wide berth, as was the habit of all wild animals in that region. Farms always come equipped with cats and dogs, and both will just as soon kill you as look at you, if you are a small

prey animal like Ben and Shoshanna. And the stallion, though
he was no small prey animal, knew that he was a spectacular
specimen. He didn't want any of the young farm hands to see
him; they might try to make a sport of coming after him with a
lasso. So the three left the grasslands of the valley and entered
the thick woods, where the going was slower and more difficult.

"I have an idea," said Casanova as he noted the shrew and
rabbit working hard to negotiate the fallen logs and boulders.
"How about if you two ride on my back? Save your energy for
the Badlands. I hear it's pretty *bad* out there." And he let out a
guffaw at his little joke.

"You know," said Ben thoughtfully, "I think you have hit
on a great idea. But how will we get up on your back? It's so
high."

"Oh, that's no problem at all," said Casanova knowingly.
"I've already thought about that, and I think I figured it out. I
could kneel down, and you could just jump up on my back, Ben.
And little shrew, you could just climb right up by the hair of my
tail. Once you get on, you both can sit in my mane. Snag your
claws in my mane and you should be able to stay on pretty well.
Or, at least I hope so. We can try it."

Ben considered this, his right paw covering his chin. "Well,
as long as you don't break into a sudden gallop, I suppose it will
work. Otherwise, I fear I'll get thrown right off. Shoshanna will
be fine either way. She's so small and light, she can bury herself
in your mane and stay on no matter what."

Casanova laughed. "All right, little rabbit. Don't be afraid.
Let's just give it a try. I promise that I won't break into a gallop
without warning you."

He kneeled on the forest floor.

The shrew scurried right up the horse's tail.

"Oo hoo! A ha ha ha!" giggled Casanova. "That tickles!
Oo hoo ha ha!"

Ben then gave a powerful thrust of his hind legs and leaped
high in the air, landing squarely on the horse's sleek back. He

nearly slid right off and would have fallen over the other side, but he somehow managed to hang on by sinking his claws into the stallion's coat.

"Oof. Ow," said Casanova, and the skin of his back twitched under Ben's sharp claws.

"Oh, goodness. So sorry," said Ben. "I had to use my claws just for a moment, to get purchase."

"Of course, of course, no problem at all," said Casanova reassuringly. "I completely understand. I'd have done the same, had I been in your place."

Shoshanna laughed aloud.

"What?" asked Ben.

"I was picturing him in your place, and you in his. A horse riding on a rabbit's back! Tee hee hee!"

"All right, you two. Enough joking around," said Casanova sternly, but there was also the sound of a smile in his voice. "Get up higher on my neck and into my mane. We really should get moving again."

He glanced nervously this way and that as he said this. Animals accustomed to life in the open field aren't as comfortable in the deep woods where the wolf, the bear, and the mountain lion lurk.

The horse remained kneeling and lay as still as possible while the two small animals crept up his back and into his mane. The shrew wrapped some strands of hair around the knuckles of her forepaws. The rabbit sank his claws into the mane and clenched a thick strand of it between his teeth. No longer able to speak, Ben nodded the go-ahead signal to Shoshanna.

"We're ready," said Shoshanna.

As the horse rose to his feet, Ben's stomach lurched. While the horse had been kneeling, Ben had already felt like he was atop a mountain, and now he was rising even higher. He squeezed his eyes shut, suddenly remembering how much he hated heights.

After rising to his full height, the horse stood very still and asked, "How are you guys doing? You both okay? Still up there?”

“Yes,” said Shoshanna, glancing over at Ben, who nodded. “We’re both doing fine.”

“All right. I’m going to start moving now,” said Casanova. “I’m going to walk slowly at first, to let you get used to it. Let’s make sure everything works all right.”

“Okay,” said Shoshanna.

The horse began plodding slowly through the woods.

“Everything okay?” he asked after a time.

“Great!” shouted Shoshanna.

“I’m good,” mumbled Ben around his mouthful of mane.

“You sound weird,” said Casanova.

Ben spit out the hair. “That’s because I’ve been hanging onto your mane with my teeth. But actually, I feel pretty solid now. I don’t think I need to bite your mane anymore. I’m right in the center of your back, so I feel balanced. I don’t think I’ll fall off.”

“Well, just be ready to bite my mane again, in case I have to run all of a sudden. And I’ll try to warn you before that happens,” said Casanova.

“Okay,” said Ben.

It took some time for Ben to fully relax and enjoy the view from his new height, but he finally did. Shoshanna, on the other hand, was almost instantly comfortable with the ride.

“Magnificent,” murmured Ben as he peered all around.

“What?” asked Shoshanna.

“All this,” said Ben, waving a forepaw at the forest in general. “It looks completely different from this height, doesn’t it?”

“It certainly does,” said Shoshanna. “I’m seeing all sorts of things I never noticed before.”

“Yes. Like the pattern the tops of the ferns make. They make big circly flower shapes.”

“Exactly! And did you notice that their tops are lighter in color than their bottoms?”

“Yes! I did see that.”

"And look how far ahead you can see," she said excitedly. "Way, way, *way* over there!"

The two couldn't see Casanova's facial expression, of course, but it showed that he was *very* pleased to be hearing this conversation.

In fact, the horse was realizing he was experiencing a brand new feeling he had never had in his entire life. It was happiness. Oh, he had been *happy* plenty of times before. But this was a different kind of happiness. This was not the happiness he had when he felt like kicking his hind legs high in the air, or when he challenged another stallion and won the mare of his desire. No, this was the unique pleasure that can only come from making *others* happy. It was a novel sensation for Casanova, and he was determined to have more of it.

"Would you two like some nuts?" asked Casanova.

"Oh, that would be lovely right about now," breathed Shoshanna.

Casanova stopped under the branch of a tree. He reached up and grasped the branch between his teeth, then shook it mightily. A shower of nuts fell on the horse and its riders.

"Oof!" said Ben, covering his head with his front paws.

"Oh!" said Shoshanna, darting for cover under the curl where the horse's thick mane flopped over to one side.

"Ah. Gee. I'm sorry," muttered the embarrassed Casanova as the shower finally petered out. "I keep forgetting how small you guys are. I hope you didn't get hurt."

"No problem," said Ben graciously. "We weren't hurt at all, were we, Shoshanna?"

"Nope!" she said brightly, emerging from her horse-hair cave.

"Did you manage to catch any nuts?" asked the horse.

"Well, *we* weren't able to catch them, but your *mane* caught plenty," said Shoshanna.

Six or seven of the nuts were still lying in the rough hair. Shoshanna began breaking open the nuts with her sharp teeth and sharing the meat with Ben.

"Well, these are delicious," said Ben through a mouthful. "Thank you, Casanova."

Casanova beamed as he plodded carefully through the forest. "You're very welcome."

Eventually, the light ahead of them changed. It wasn't like the cool shade of the deep forest they had been passing through. Just ahead lay bright and sunny patches, and beyond that, a glimpse of blue sky. All three animals instinctively grew still and silent.

"Is that a large clearing, or a meadow, maybe?" whispered Casanova.

"Or the end of the forest entirely?" suggested Shoshanna in a low voice.

"Only one way to find out," said Ben.

"Hang on tight, you two. Ben, you'd better bite my mane right now. Who knows what we'll find out there," whispered Casanova. "And, if it's a safe and wide open space, my legs will probably take us for a good hard sprint, anyhow. I can't always help it. My legs sometimes just start running before I can stop them."

"Hey, when you gotta stretch, you gotta stretch," said Ben understandingly. "That's just instinct."

He took a big bite of Casanova's mane between his teeth.

"M'kay," said Ben.

"Ben is ready, Casanova," Shoshanna added helpfully.

Casanova took in a breath so deep that his sides expanded, then let it out slowly. "All right. Let's go."

Ben gratefully realized that Casanova was actually moving in a prudent and cautious manner, rather than darting out into the open like a wild fool.

Well, good for him, thought Ben. *Maybe he's finally realized that he doesn't actually know it all, and he's not really invincible— at least, not way out here in unfamiliar territory.*

Casanova moved quietly toward the bright light, remaining

as long as possible under the shade of the large trees. But the trees quickly became shorter, more scraggly. Their leaves, too, changed from lush and dark green to small and yellowy-green, so there was far less cover in which to hide. Finally, the horse had no choice but to step fully, nakedly, out into the light. Standing with the backdrop of the forest behind him, he stood very still as the three tried to get a good look at the lay of the land ahead.

What they saw was a land layered in all the colors of the sunset. Brown, tan, gold, orange, pink and red. It was magnificent, but other-worldly. They saw not a bit of green. In fact, the last bit of shrubbery they stood among, coming barely to the height of the stallion's shoulders, was no longer a true green, at least, not what they would have called "green" back home in the meadow. No, this green was a drab grayish olive. And the leaves on these stunted bushes were thick, stiff, and tiny, as if they were skittish about revealing their full lushness in that harsh environment.

"Oh!" said Casanova as his coat brushed hard against one of the bushes. "Those branches are tough and spiny. Ow! Oh, I don't like that." His skin twitched, and he performed one of those odd, cross-legged side steps away from the bush, the kind of movement which might get a horse mistaken for a good tap dancer.

Shoshanna, in the meantime, had been working her nostrils ferociously, her mouthful of sharp teeth gaped wide open in her effort to pick up scents.

"Seems safe enough to proceed," she concluded with a sharp nod. "Every scent smells pretty old around here, except for maybe those of a few smaller animals my own size. Nothing dangerous. What do you two think?"

Both horse and rabbit sniffed for a good long time.

"Let's move out," said Casanova.

"Agreed," said Ben.

Ben and Shoshanna had already decided to sit with their backs to one another, so as to better keep watch. Ben faced the rear to watch for any crouching, creeping predator, like a mountain lion. Shoshanna faced the front. Her nose was actually much better than her sight, but she used her eyes as well. Her nostrils quivered constantly, taking in any odors carried on the stilting, stifling breeze. And Casanova, who had one eye situated on each side of his face, was perfectly equipped to watch their left and right flanks simultaneously.

Carefully they descended down, down, down into the sandy desert valley. Almost immediately they had their first miserable encounter with a cactus, when Casanova's flank carelessly brushed one of its spines.

"Oh! Oh! Ow! Ow! Ow!" moaned Casanova pitifully. He tried to twist his head around and grab the thing that was stuck in his flank with his teeth, but could not. "What in the world *is* that burning thing?"

"Hold still," said Shoshanna. "Try to stay calm and quiet. Let's not attract attention to ourselves. We are sitting ducks out here." Her eyes darted this way and that. She listened. There was neither noise nor movement, apart from the bits of dry sand spilling gently down the dunes whenever the wind stirred.

"I have an idea," she said after a long, quiet moment. "Ben, hold my hind legs and lower me down to the spiny thing. I think I can pull it out with my teeth."

Casanova clenched his jaw at such a thought, but remained very still.

Ben lowered Shoshanna over the side of the horse's back. Shoshanna braced her little paws against the horse's flank, then sank her teeth into the cactus spine. Shrews are famously strong and fierce for their size. And they don't ever give up. Shoshanna pulled and pulled and pulled, straining her neck and back mightily, until the spine came loose. She spit it out and it tumbled to the ground, along with four droplets of Casanova's blood. Shoshanna quickly licked the horse's wound until the bleeding stopped.

"Ah... ah... much better. Thank you. Thank you," said Casanova.

Ben frowned. "We have spilled some blood on the ground.

It won't be long before predators smell it and come after us. Shall we gallop, Casanova?"

Casanova shook his head. "I'll not gallop through this place, not if I don't want to catch another spiny thing in my flank... or, worse yet, in the center of my hoof!" He shuddered. "But I will certainly *trot*. Hang on, you two!"

Ben bit hard into a portion of the horse's mane, and Shoshanna wrapped her strong claws in its hair.

Off they went across the hot, dry valley, surrounded by nothing but rocks, sand and cacti. For three hours, the scenery went on just like that.

"*Bah*. I don't *like* this," splurted Casanova.

"Do you suppose *this* is the Badlands of Badness?" murmured Shoshanna, her bright eyes staring all around. "Because it certainly is quite unpleasant."

"I vote 'yes,'" said Ben.

A few hours more, and the animals realized they were exceedingly thirsty.

"We must find shade," said Casanova. "My coat is black, so this heat is really getting to me."

Shoshanna, who was already sheltering in the shade of the horse's flopped-over mane, said, "Well, I'm sweltering even under here, so I can't imagine how *you* must feel. Please do try and get closer to those tall rocky things in the distance. They look shady enough."

There were some tall rocks in the shapes of odd pillars dotted here and there throughout the landscape. They looked close, but when the horse headed for a group of them, the animals soon discovered the illusory nature of distant objects in the Badlands of Badness.

"It's gonna take forever to get over there," panted the horse.

"And will we ever find any water in this horrid place?" asked Ben, a note of real fear entering his voice for the first time in their adventure.

Shoshanna closed her eyes. She took in the oven-hot air deeply, then nodded to herself. "I have just asked the Maker to help us. He says he will. He says we are in exactly the right place." She breathed again, eyes still closed. "I see... I see two tall rocky things. I see us standing in front of them."

Ben let out a sigh of relief. Shoshanna had a way of hearing the Maker that most other animals didn't. She saw things most other animals didn't see. That made her very dear and special to him, among her other qualities of kindness and generosity. And Ben knew the Maker well. If he had told Shoshanna something, you could believe it. He always told the truth.

Casanova, however, felt no such relief.

"How do you know?" he asked in something akin to a pitiful whine. "I mean, I *hope* you are right, Shoshanna, but... How do you *know* the Maker really said that to you? He *never* talks to me."

Shoshanna considered her answer carefully. "I know, because I know that voice. I just... know."

"Huh," said the horse, half skeptically, half wistfully. "Wish I could know him the way you do."

"Oh, you can," said Shoshanna.

"Really?"

"Oh, yes. Anyone can. That's what the Maker loves to do. Talk to us."

"So I've heard," mused Casanova. "What about you, Ben? Does he talk to you?"

Ben had to really think hard about this answer. *Did* the Maker ever talk to him?

Finally, Ben spit out his mouthful of mane and said, "He does, but not in the same way that he talks to Shoshanna. I... sort of... feel him. And I know what he expects of me. And I try to do it. I do know that he loves me."

"Huh," said Casanova, almost to himself.

Ben again picked up the bit of mane with his teeth.

The three fell silent as they half-trotted, half plodded through the alternately sandy and rocky terrain, always heading for the tall rocky pillars that looked close but were actually far.

"HISSSS!!! YA! YA! YA! BACK, BACK, BACK with YA!"

The snarling voice from below came completely without warning. Casanova let out a shrieking neigh and reared up on hind legs so that he was almost fully vertical. Then he skittered and hopped backward about eight feet. Thankfully, both Ben and Shoshanna managed to remain atop the horse, but only barely.

"What was *that?*" muttered Casanova to his two friends.

All three scanned the sand-strewn ground ahead, but saw nothing.

Nothing, that is, until the sand *moved*.

And up from the sand emerged the largest, most golden crawdad any of them had ever seen. Except *this* crawdad had a long tail which curled up over its back, equipped with a fearsome spike.

"It's one of those land crawdads from the stories..." breathed Ben.

"With fiery death in its tail..." quoted Shoshanna in a whisper.

The thing shouted and emitted a rattling hiss. "I *heard* that!" He came scuttling rapidly toward the horse's hooves, waving claws and tail menacingly. "You *dare* to insult me?!"

Casanova quickly jumped back up another two feet.

"Sorry, Mr. Crawdad," said Casanova. "We don't mean to offend."

"ARRHHH!!!" said the crawdad, racing forward again. "Say it again, and see if I don't kill you *all*, here and now, with the great power of my tail! See what a painful death awaits you!"

"What did we say? What did we say?" asked Shoshanna. "We're so sorry!"

The fear and humility in her voice caused the crawdad to strain his beady eyes to search for her atop the horse's mane. He must have sensed her genuine dismay and sorrow, for his claws lowered slowly to the ground.

"You folks aren't from around these parts, are you?" he said.

"No, sir," said Casanova.

"Well, then, let me school you three just a bit. I am not a *land crawdad*, as some of you foreigners like to call us. No, *sir*. I am a *scorpion*. And right proud of it."

"No offense intended," said Ben. "We are very sorry. We didn't know what you were called. And we didn't even know you were real."

The scorpion laughed his dry, dusty laugh, a laugh that sounded like Mexican jumping beans rattling in a tin. "Of *course* we're real. Now, wait a minute. I've always wondered something myself. Are *crawdads* real, then? The legends say that they swim in deep puddles of water that never go dry. And they don't have a nice big tail like me."

"Oh, yes. Crawdads are real. They look sort of like you, but they are smaller, with no big tail. And they are not golden and pretty like you," said Shoshanna thoughtfully.

If scorpions had the capability of smiling, this one would have, out of sheer delight. Not all scorpions are malicious (though many are). However, they are all notoriously vain, and thus susceptible to the least bit of flattery. Shoshanna's sincere compliment had unwittingly put her on this scorpion's good side.

"Well, I *am* told that my exoskeleton has a *particularly* golden hue. But I don't have good vision, so I'll admit that I've been forced to take other people's word for it," chuckled the scorpion. "Really?" he hummed pleasurably, attempting to arch himself to get a better look at his own back. "Do you *really* think I look *golden?*"

Casanova was quickly becoming irritated at the scorpion's vanity. It was rubbing him the wrong way. He couldn't understand why it rubbed him the wrong way, and the fact that he couldn't understand why was also bothering him. If Shoshanna and Ben had had the opportunity to counsel him privately on the matter, they would have told Casanova that he was now witnessing, in vivid display, an undesirable trait in the scorpion which Casanova himself frequently exhibited. Inwardly, Casanova despised such vanity within himself, but he had practiced it for so many years that he could no longer perceive the moments that he indulged in it. Seeing it held up like a mirror in front of his face was more than he could take.

"Er, um, Mr. Scorpion, speaking of puddles," interjected Casanova impatiently. "We are *super* thirsty. Could you perhaps be so kind as to direct us to some water?"

"Why, sure. It's all over the place!" said the scorpion, waving its pincers as though the answer was obvious.

"I... I don't see it," said the bewildered horse, looking this way and that.

"Just grab yourself a nice, fat insect or a grub, and there ya go!" rattled the scorpion, clicking off a cool snap of his right pincer on the word 'go.' "All the water you need. Now, you might need to dig down a little to find 'em. But you know the old saying, 'If ya don't work, ya don't eat.'"

Shoshanna nodded in agreement, but Ben and Casanova weren't so gung ho.

"Ah. Yes. Thank you," said Ben politely. "That's all well and good for a shrew like Shoshanna. But I am a rabbit, you see, and Casanova here is a horse. We don't eat bugs... not unless it's the absolute last resort. We eat plants, seeds, vegetables, fruits, grains... you know, that sort of thing."

"Huh?" asked the scorpion. He turned his beady eyes quizzically to Shoshanna and raised both pincers in a helpless shrug. "What the heck are they talking about?"

"Um, Mr. Scorpion," smiled Shoshanna. "I guess our real question is, is there a puddle nearby?"

"Nope. Not right now. Gotta wait for the next time water comes down from the sky."

"Ah. I see. And when will that be, in your estimation?"

"Oh, not long. Not long at all. Maybe two more moons, I'm guessing. That's when we get lots of water. BIG puddles. Rushing all down between the cliffs and such, and then piling up at the bottom." He spread out his claws and made wide circles with them in the air, attempting to illustrate just how big the puddles could get.

Two more months? The shrew and the rabbit, still resting atop the horse's back, turned to stare at each other in silent horror. They heard Casanova make a small, audible gasp. They all knew that they surely could not survive two months without water.

"Oh! Gotta go!" said the scorpion suddenly. "Hear that? Wife's rattlin' for me. And you know what they say... 'Happy wife, happy life!'" Then a pained, dark look overshadowed his tiny face. He sighed, and his lateral eyes drooped earthward. "Don't want her to get too mad at me. Don't feel like getting eaten tonight." He let out a pathetic, nervous chuckle.

In an instant, he had hidden himself completely back under the sand and was presumably skittering down the tunnel of his cool underground lair.

"Oh, *my*," said Ben. "That's... well, that's *awful*. Just think what poor Mr. Scorpion's domestic life is like!"

"Yeah. You know, he reminds me of a spider husband I once knew back home," said Shoshanna ruefully. "They're all bluff and bluster when they're out and about, but once they get home, they really have to mind their p's and q's."

Casanova tossed his mane disdainfully. "Not in *my* harem. *I'm* the boss of *my* harem."

Ben smiled to himself and said aloud, "That so? How many do you have in your harem, Casanova?"

The stallion snorted once and paused. He dropped his head and pretended to sniff the ground. "Well, what I *meant* to say was, *when* I have a harem. *One* day. *That's* when I'll be the boss."

"Ah," said Ben gently and kindly. "Yes. Yes. I'm sure you will, Casanova."

The horse lifted his head again to scan the horizon, pointing his nose and ears toward the towering, distant rocks.

"You see that?" asked Casanova. "Out there. The air above the ground looks wavy and wobbly, like it's all under water." He sniffed the breeze. "But there's no water out that way.

"Huh," said Ben, narrowing his eyes to focus on the spot. "That's pretty peculiar. I never did see the like in all my days."

Shoshanna looked at the wavy place for a long time. "I don't *think* it's anything to worry about," she said. "My gut is telling me to just press on."

Had the three of them grown up in an arid desert climate, they would have known that they were seeing heat waves rising up from the ground, creating refraction in the air. Some call it heat haze, some call it a mirage. Whatever you call it, it made the three animals feel vaguely unsettled. Any new environment or phenomenon can do that to anyone.

Before the horse began his half plod, half trot toward the rocky columns, he asked the tough question they all were asking themselves. "Do you guys really believe we should go that far out, not knowing if we'll ever find any water? Maybe we should turn back."

Ben waited to see what Shoshanna would say, and her answer both surprised and encouraged him.

"We absolutely do not turn back," said Shoshanna firmly, shaking her head side to side. "The one thing I was able to see in my mind the last time I spoke with the Maker was that the three of us were standing before two tall rocks, and I knew that something good was beyond them."

"Something good?" protested Casanova. "But, the squirrels said that the birds told them there was nothing but the Worselands of Worseness beyond the Badlands of Badness. And I just don't think I can go another day without water."

Ben climbed higher on the horse's neck and put his mouth against Casanova's twitching ear. "You can trust Shoshanna in this," he whispered. "Don't worry. She's never been wrong about this sort of thing. And I have a good feeling about it, too, as though the Maker would be happy if we went forward rather than backward.”

The horse’s shoulders relaxed a bit. “Okay. If you two feel confident about going forward, then I want to continue, too.” He let out a low chuckle. “Besides, where’s the adventure in turning around and running for home?”

“*That’s* the spirit!” cheered Ben, and Shoshanna smiled calmly, now staring at two particularly tall and prominent natural stone columns in the distance.

All along the way, they suffered in the intense heat, both from the beating sun above and the sparkling white-hot sands below. More than once the shrew and the rabbit expressed their gratitude to Casanova for carrying them and sparing their paw pads some severe burns.

“Ah, I’m glad to do it. That’s what hooves are good for,” said Casanova, but the cottony way his mouth sounded when he said it made the smaller animals worry about how parched he must be. He did seem to sweat mightily under the blazing sun, even though the dry air wicked it away quickly.

They traveled for at least two more hours in this manner, seeing no other company than the occasional tarantula, snake or lizard, who either spoke to them in such a strange tongue that they couldn’t understand, or else darted out of sight without so much as a friendly nod their way.

Yes, the Badlands of Badness were very bad indeed. No water. No ample shade. Nothing to eat. And, worst of all, no kindness or hospitality. Even the scorpion with whom they had briefly conversed had at first accosted them with harsh threats. He had only deigned to speak civilly to them after he had been flattered by Shoshanna’s compliment on his golden exoskeleton.

Finally, mercifully, they arrived, parched and faint, at the foot of the two natural pillars of stone.

Casanova instantly trotted into the darkest shade cast by the pillars and leaned his flank against that portion of the rock, which had retained a remnant of coolness from the frigid temperatures of the night prior.

"Ahhhh..." said the horse, closing his eyes in delight and pressing hard against the rock.

"What a relief!" said Shoshanna, emerging from under Casanova's mane.

Even in the shade, the temperature had to be in the low nineties, but the comfort the shade provided, as compared to the merciless glare of the direct sun, was substantial.

"Who... ssseeksss... the Sssseven?" uttered a voice.

The voice was so sharply sibilant that it felt to the animals to be slicing their eardrums.

The blood of all three mammals ran cold, and each instinctively froze in a state of temporary paralysis. Never in their lives had they heard a voice so potent, so ominous. So predatory. And yet, at the same time, so very *charming*.

Casanova recovered the use of his four legs and turned his body to face the opening between the tall rocky pillars. Ben and Shoshanna peeked cautiously over the horse's mane and between his ears.

"Who... sseeksssss... the Sssseven?" the enchanting voice repeated, this time in a tone more silken, less booming, almost coaxing.

Perhaps it would be better to call what they heard "voices" rather than "a voice." There was a sort of multiplicity about the sound, as though several entities were speaking in unison, or—better—as though a single mind were speaking through several mouths at once.

"We don't know who the Seven are, sirs," said Casanova as bravely as he could. "We are just three travelers who have traveled far from home. We are looking for water, sirs. Do you know where we might find some water?"

Shoshanna, Ben and Casanova each wondered privately why they felt their very bones shaking within them as they scanned the space between the pillars, from where the voice seemed to be coming.

The voice—or voices—emitted a chuckle very pleasing to the ear, yet tainted with the faintest hint of—what? Mockery?

"Water?" it said. "Oh, my dear little friends. Tsk, tsk, tsk. You are a long, long way from water."

With that, the body of an enormous red serpent came roiling and coiling out of the space between the columns, filling up the gap with its tremendous girth and length. Rising up from that body, to a height of ten or twelve feet, were seven serpent heads, eyes fixed on the three friends. Seven tongues flickered in and out like slender red flames.

All three animals' mouths gaped in awe at the massive serpent. Never had they seen or heard of such a large snake, not even in the stories of the migrating birds who hailed from the great river jungles of the southern continents. And never had they seen or heard of any animal with *seven heads.*

For all seven heads indeed shared the same serpent body.
The Seven.

The creature was a marvel, and the three found they couldn't tear their eyes from the creature, not only for its majestic beauty and strength, but also for the perverse disgust it engendered, a disgust that seemed to choke in their throats and hold them frozen like statues, while the thing coiled and uncoiled, making its dry, hypnotic scraping sounds across the dusty rock. From time to time, one of the serpent heads would slowly extend toward them in mid-air, approaching to get a closer look at the horse's face, while at the same time another head would loop around the back of the horse to investigate the scents of the smaller mammals by gently flicking at their fur with a forked tongue. It was a terrifying ordeal, but Casanova, Ben and Shoshanna all knew deep within their hearts that there would be no outrunning, outfighting, or outsmarting *this* predator. There was nothing for them to do but remain perfectly still and try to survive the stomach-churning encounter.

"What are your names, my young guesssssstssss?" asked all

seven heads simultaneously.

Ben was the one to clear his throat this time. "I am Ben. And these are my friends, Shoshanna and Casanova. And you, sirs? Are you the Seven?"

"We are, we are," said the serpent. "Now. What brings you this way, so very, very far from your home?"

"We are explorers," said Casanova. "We seek to know what lies beyond the Badlands of Badness."

"Hmm...." said the serpent. "Well. *That* is certainly very interesting. And where is this Badlands of Badness of which you sssspeak?"

Shoshanna and Ben looked at each other uncertainly and remained quiet.

But Casanova protested, "Why, it is right here! It's where we are right now!"

The serpent threw back all seven heads at once and laughed heartily, a sonorous belly laugh that shook the ground and yet still felt hollow, as if devoid of any real joy at its core.

"This land is *good*," said the serpent. "It is very, very good! You three are mistaken."

"*No*, sir," squeaked Shoshanna, shaking her head firmly. "It is *not* a good land. Maybe it is good for snakes, tarantulas and scorpions. But it is not good for *us*."

"But, oh, my dear child, yes, it *is* good for you. Very, *very* good. Look again. Tell me what you see." All seven heads lifted up and focused at something in the distance behind them, back the way they had just come.

The three turned around and scanned the terrain. Not far off, they saw a beautiful green oasis with a crystal clear pool fed by a sparkling waterfall. Trees laden with ripe fruit gleamed in the sunshine.

Casanova didn't even stop to think. "Water!" he shouted.

Instantly he galloped straight for the oasis, carrying Ben and Shoshanna with him, whether they wanted it or not. But as soon as he arrived—now panting and covered with dust—at the place where he was positive it had just been, the oasis had somehow vanished from sight.

"What?" asked Casanova, turning his head left and right. "Where...?"

"There! There!" shouted Ben excitedly as he pointed at something three hundred yards ahead.

But Shoshanna was frowning.

Casanova bolted straight for the spring's new location, calling over his shoulder, "I think I must have turned the wrong way back there at that big cactus. But *now* we're on the right track!"

They came around a tall dune, fully expecting to find the oasis, but saw nothing. However, shimmering just beyond another distant rock formation, a spring of delicious blue water danced before their eyes. Yes. There again was that green grass, that lovely orchard.

Casanova was just about to dash toward the spot one more time when Shoshanna shouted, "Stop! Stop, everyone! Something isn't right. Stop. Let's think about this!"

Shoshanna rarely raised her voice in this manner, so Casanova halted in his tracks.

Ben spoke up. "You know what? Shoshanna's right. Something feels 'off' about this thing."

Shoshanna waved her tiny paws back in the direction of the rocky columns. "Look how far we are from the place the Maker told us to go!" she said in great dismay. "It took all our strength to get there the first time, too! And, Casanova, can't you see how your sides are heaving? You are wasting your precious last reserves. We *need* to stay alive. Now, whatever these things are that we have been chasing, wouldn't you agree that none of them have turned out to be what they ought to be, or where they ought to be?"

"I think you must be right," said Ben pensively. But, almost in spite of himself, his eyes remained fixed on the gorgeous emerald oasis. It still seemed to be right *there*, almost within reach.

"I... I'm just not sure," said Casanova. "You know what? I honestly think I didn't try hard enough on the first two attempts. I must have gotten myself all confused and lost my bearings. But *this* time... *this* time... I do believe we can make it!" He took two steps toward the oasis and strained his neck in its direction.

"Wait!" shouted Shoshanna.

Casanova halted again.

She made a strenuous effort to calm her tone. "Even if it *is* a perfectly good oasis with real water and good food and all of that," she said, "it's *still* not the place the Maker told us to go. He showed me that we needed to get past the tall columns. And look! There they are behind us now! The two tall columns from the picture he showed me are way back over there!"

She waved her forelegs frantically toward the rear of the horse, toward the columns, but only Ben could see her from his vantage point on the horse's back. Casanova could not see her. He could only hear Shoshanna, and perhaps this drawback was contributing to the strong temptation he was now facing. His eyes were so fixed on the loveliness of the oasis scene ahead, he almost couldn't bear it for the yearning it engendered in his heart.

"CASANOVA. TURN AROUND. NOW!" commanded Shoshanna with an authority Ben had only heard her wield against her most mischievous offspring.

Casanova sighed, but obeyed. He reluctantly turned himself around to face the tall rocky columns. "All right, all right, all right," he muttered. "I guess we'll do it *Shoshanna's* way."

Ben felt a tiny arrow pierce his heart, as the former unity of their friendship was torn by that statement, even if just a little.

Shoshanna sighed and allowed her voice to resolve to its usual sweet gentleness.

"Not *my* way, Casanova," she said quietly. "The *Maker's* way."

Casanova stood still and said nothing. He stared stonily,

straight ahead at the rocks.

"Do you understand what I mean by that, Casanova?" she asked.

"I do," he sighed. His head bowed. "You are right, I suppose. I just don't *like* it."

"No, I don't either. Sometimes it is hard to obey the Maker's signs and pictures. It is not always very comfortable."

"You're right. I'm starting to see that it's not," said the horse.

"But it always works out just right," she added encouragingly, her tone lifting in cheerful hope.

Casanova remained stationary.

Ben nudged Shoshanna and gave her a look that said, *Let me try.*

"Casanova," he said, "do you remember when we first thought about riding on your back? When we were in the forest? Shoshanna and I were a little nervous to try it at first. We didn't know how it would work out. And so we had to learn to trust you. But it has turned out really great. You knew where to go and how to put your hooves down in the right spots. You got us through the woods and down the ravines and over the sand and the rocks, and no one fell down or got hurt. In fact, I'm positive we two would have *died* without you carrying us on this journey."

Casanova let a small puff through his nostrils and lowered his head yet more.

"So," Ben continued, "I think, in just the same way, the Maker is saying it is time that *you* learn how to ride on *his* back."

The horse slowly lifted his head, as if a brand new concept was gradually forming in his mind.

"Ohhh... I see. I see it now," said Casanova. "Well... I can do *that*."

For, you see, somewhere along that tiresome and taxing journey, Casanova had had a personal revelation, and it was that revelation which was allowing him to comprehend this new concept of trust. He had learned that the Maker was a real

Somebody and not just a make-pretend person. Somewhere along the way, Casanova had come to believe that an animal like himself really could begin to trust the Maker.

Now, if you were to try to pin Casanova down and ask him exactly how and when he had come to know this so deeply and so certainly, he wouldn't be able to explain it to you. It is this writer's opinion that Casanova met the Maker inside his own heart as he was crossing that horrible desert and looking for water... but no one can say for sure. No one, that is, except for Casanova himself.

At this point, Casanova finally had the right attitude and was ready to head back to the two stone columns. But by the time the stallion had plodded all the way back to the pillars, the three animals were all the more exhausted and parched. Casanova was actually trembling with fatigue. Ben's eyes were making everything look fuzzy. Shoshanna was gasping in the heat, taking in the hot, dry air with sharp, shallow breaths.

The space between the columns was empty when they arrived.

"Looks like that serpent thing is gone," said Casanova. "I'm gonna go for it."

He headed for the opening.

But in an instant, the fearsome snake reappeared and filled the space between the columns with its massive coils.

"You've returned?" came the seven voices, politely enough, but ever so faintly tinged with displeasure and impatience.

"We have returned, and we intend to go through. Please let us pass," said Shoshanna.

"No. I'm sorry, but I cannot let you pass," said the serpent.

"And why not?" demanded Casanova, his right forehoof pawing at the hot dust.

"Because. I truly do not wish to see the three of you come to harm. The land ahead is... shall we say... rather inhospitable."

"We have been told by the Maker to go forward," persisted Shoshanna.

"The *Maker?*" chuckled the serpent. "Oh, really? He said that, did he? And do you always do *everything* that the Maker suggests you do?"

"We do," said Shoshanna simply and sincerely. "And he didn't just *suggest*. He *commanded*."

Ben and Casanova nodded firmly in agreement.

"Well, I suppose it's *your* lives that are at stake," said the serpent pityingly. "I mean, it really is *your* choice, after all. We all have free will, of course. To each his own."

"Wait a minute. What are you trying to say?" demanded Casanova, glaring at the Seven with narrowed eyes.

"Don't, Casanova," warned Shoshanna in a hushed voice.

But it was too late. The horse had taken the bait, and the Seven knew it. The serpent fixed all fourteen of its deadly eyes on Casanova's face. "Well, all that I'm trying to say, my dear equine friend, is simply this. Here you are, having followed the Maker's advice all the way out here. And there has been no water, has there? There has been no food, either. There has been no shade. The Maker hasn't exactly kept a good record so far, has he? And you do realize that the terrain only gets much, much worse when you go past this point." He chuckled quietly, almost to himself. He shook his heads. "I mean, it *does* seem a bit of a fool's errand, doesn't it?"

Casanova remained silent and chewed on this statement.

Shoshanna spoke up. "It's never a fool's errand to obey the Master."

"Yes, yes, yes, little shrew," said the serpent condescendingly, closing all of its eyes for a moment and nodding all seven heads. "Of course. I suppose you *could* be right about that. But, after all, what is the *point* of the excursion? Is it not reasonable to ask how it *benefits* anyone? Indeed, you might ask: what benefit is there in it for *you*?"

Casanova pawed the ground anxiously, uncertainly.

It was then that a fierce look stole over Shoshanna's face— one that Ben recognized as the expression she had when she defended her babies from predators who came too close to her nest.

"Casanova, let's go," she said firmly through clenched teeth.

"But—"

"NOW!" she commanded.

The serpent remained calmly in position, calling out to them as they retreated. "There is no other way through, you realize." Then it laughed to itself, shaking its head at the supposed folly of the three travelers.

Once out of earshot of the beast, the three conferred in whispers.

"We can't go through the space between the pillars as long as that serpent is there, so we must try to find another way around," said Shoshanna.

"Agreed," whispered Ben.

Casanova remained silent.

"Casanova? You okay? Something wrong?" asked Ben.

"Well... it's just... I don't know. It kinda bothered me what he said about the Maker. I was just wondering if what he said might be... might be just a *little* true. Do you think maybe the Maker left us out here and forgot about us? Not that he would *mean* to do that, but...by mistake? And then I have to wonder. Why are we even out here, so far away from any water?"

Shoshanna sighed. "Casanova, everything that miserable snake said is just a lie. The Maker never, ever leaves us. And he never makes a mistake. And as to why we are out here, I'll admit that I don't know the reason, but one thing I do know for sure, in the very center of my being, is that we are *supposed to be here*. Here's what I think you should do. Just take a moment right now to ask the Maker yourself, and you'll see that I am right about this."

The confidence in her voice seemed to revive the stallion's courage. Ben and Shoshanna waited respectfully as Casanova's head lifted and his ears twitched in the silence. He appeared to be listening hard to someone.

"You're right. That thing *was* lying to us," Casanova said. "Now that I think about it, it felt all wrong and bad and scary whenever he was talking. And now I feel much better."

"Excellent!" said Ben. "Now, let's try and find another way through. But before we set out, let me go out on a limb and say my piece right now. If the Worselands of Worseness are the only thing that we find on the other side, and if there's still no water to be found out there, then so be it. The Maker made everything that is. If the Maker wants to make brand new water for us to drink over there, even if there isn't any there right now, he can certainly do that. He can do whatever he wants."

"There you go!" said Shoshanna. "Well said. Now, Casanova, I suggest we go to the left of the pillars a little bit and see if we can circle around that serpent."

They went to the left a little way, but there the land dropped sharply down into a tall and steep canyon that they could not negotiate.

"All right," said Ben with as much cheer as he could muster, "then we go to the right instead."

To go to the right side of the columns, they would have to pass in front of the Seven again.

They did so cautiously, traveling a wide arc to stay out of striking distance of the serpent's long body.

"Ha," mocked the serpent as they passed him. "You are foolishly wasting your time and energy. I have already told you. There is no other way through."

The three animals ignored the beast, and this unfortunately aroused its ire. The Seven was also angry because his keen eyes had noted a marked shift in their demeanor. The three mammals were no longer susceptible to his charms, for they saw him for what he really was. They also seemed to have lost all fear of the serpent, at least for the time being.

Distraction hadn't worked. Deception hadn't worked. There was only one weapon remaining in the serpent's arsenal.

Destruction.

The hairs on all three animals stood straight up as they sensed the serpent's intent to attack before it lunged for them. Casanova whinnied, Ben bit down hard on the horse's mane, and the stallion bolted. Seven heads, jaws fully unhinged and fangs bared, struck at the dusty ground where the horse had been standing just a split-second before.

Casanova galloped for all his might to the right side of the stone pillars. He was running alongside a nearly vertical rock formation that blocked their way forward. But the serpent was in hot pursuit, easily keeping pace.

"Look! Look! A cleft in the rock!" shouted Shoshanna.

Casanova turned his head leftward and noticed a large vertical crack in the rock formation. The cleft was just wide and tall enough for the horse, but perhaps not large enough for the serpent's wide and massive heads to get through. Casanova darted inside, then instantly slowed his pace, for the shadowy interior made it difficult to see what lay ahead. He walked twenty steps forward into the darkness and came to a halt while he caught his breath.

"Listen," whispered Ben. "Did it follow us? Did it get in?"

They all stood still and listened. They could hear the scuttling of the serpent's scales scraping over the earth outside, back and forth, back and forth, but the sounds did not come nearer.

"I think it's too big to get in here," said Shoshanna. "I think we are safe."

"How on earth did you even see that crack in the stone, Shoshanna?" said Ben. "I barely noticed it even when Casanova was running straight for it!"

"I really don't know. I just looked, and there it was," she said.

"And as soon as you saw it, I turned my head and looked, and it appeared. I think we've just experienced a miracle," said Casanova.

"Well said, dear horse," said Ben.

The three friends conferred and concluded that they could never go back the way they had entered. So they pressed on, hoping the cleft in the stone didn't turn out to be a dead end. The darkness, which had been bad enough at the entrance, turned pitch black as they progressed, so Casanova had to carefully feel his way along. After a time, the sound of his hooves began to echo in a way that made the three think they might have entered a large cavern. Five minutes into the journey, the darkness abated and gave way to dim light, and they could see that they were indeed in a large cave. Shafts of light then started to pour in from cracks in the rocky ceiling above.

"Aha!" said Casanova brightly. "Look ahead! I think I see a way out!"

Indeed, a glimmer of blue sky was peeking through an opening in the cave wall.

Before they knew it, they had passed through the opening and were standing outside, blinking in the bright sunshine.

"Unbelievable..." breathed Ben.

But Ben's "unbelievable" was a bad "unbelievable," not a good one.

If the three had been asked to describe the scene, they wouldn't have had the terminology for it. Their limited exposure to forest, meadow and farm hadn't provided the vocabulary for *lava field, volcanic ash, basalt.* As far as their eyes could see was nothing but blackened wasteland, through which an orange river of fire flowed, amid hissing steam and gray rising smoke.

"It's the Worselands of Worseness," murmured Casanova. "Would you look at that. It's *real.* It's not just a story. It's a real place."

The three stared in silence for a solid minute.

"Well, now we'll be able to settle the squirrels' debate, once and for all," said Ben with a mirthless chuckle.

"Yeah, that's *if* we get out of here alive," said Casanova. "We *must* find some water."

"I don't see any. Don't smell any," said Ben, his whiskers bobbling furiously as he sniffed. "What about you, Shoshanna?"

She sniffed and shook her head. "I smell no water. Ach. This smoky air burns my nose."

"So... now what?" asked Casanova. "Do we turn back?"

All three remained silent, thinking their own thoughts, asking questions inside their own heads that they knew only the Maker could hear.

Do we go forward? Do we return? Is there water ahead?

Finally, Shoshanna said, "I think—I think we are supposed to go forward." She laughed shakily. "I know that seems absurd, but, there it is. That's what I really think."

Ben nodded. "I was thinking the same thing, crazy as it sounds."

"Me too!" whinnied Casanova gleefully. He was overjoyed that he was finally able to hear the right direction to go, just as his two friends had been doing all during the journey.

So forward they went.

But this part of their travels was toughest of all. The black stone which covered the ground was still piping hot in some spots, and only marginally cooler in others, for the baking sun heated even the hardened lava to a searing degree. Casanova had to carefully pick out which places were safe for his hooves, and those places were few and far between. Sometimes he gave up trying to find a good passage and galloped painfully across the scalding hot stone.

Shoshanna and Ben constantly scanned the horizon, looking for any hopeful signs of water or vegetation, but there was none. All they could see was more black stone, flowing over the land with its alien, charred shapes of static currents and eddies.

The terrain went on this way for an hour, when Shoshanna suddenly said, "I think we are supposed to go to the right."

This they did, and it took them in the direction of a distant mesa which was hard to see at first amid the rising steam and smoke. It took another hour to get close to it, by which time the blackened stone had finally given way to sand dunes and scraggly desert plants. The three friends never thought they would be so glad to see a cactus again. The sight of *anything* living brought at least a little cheer to their exhausted spirits.

"Is that a passage?" asked Ben, peering at a crack in the side of the mesa.

"Looks like it," panted Casanova. "But before we explore it, can we rest? I'm really feeling faint. Honestly, I don't think I can walk another step right now."

All three animals paused and fell silent, just as they had before. They listened carefully inside their hearts for the voice of the Maker.

"As soon as you feel rested, Casanova, I think it is good that we go into that passage," said Shoshanna.

"I feel the same way," said Ben. "But you rest first, Casanova."

Casanova stood in the shade of the mesa, closed his eyes and drifted off.

Ben and Shoshanna glanced at each other with some concern.

"There had better be water on the other side of that passage," said Ben.

Shoshanna frowned and nodded. She talked to the Maker in her heart, asking him to give Casanova an extra bit of strength.

When Casanova awoke a half hour later, he was very stiff but said he felt better. His tongue was sticking inside his mouth, so it was hard for the others to understand his words. But still he plodded faithfully onward, straight into the passage.

The rocks rose up like tall cliffs on either side of the stallion, sometimes narrowing so much that Casanova's sides scraped uncomfortably against the stone. But eventually, after a particularly sharp turn in the path, the most wonderful sound and smell in the entire world struck the three animals square in the face.

"A waterfall!" shouted Ben. "That's a *waterfall!* I'd know that sound anywhere!"

The sound was faint, but it was unmistakable. So was the scent of water.

"WOO HOO!" shouted Casanova, picking up the pace.

"Careful, careful," laughed Shoshanna. "You don't know what's around the next curve, Casanova. Just watch your footing. We'll get there soon enough."

They wound their way along the serpentine passage until it suddenly burst open into a clearing, displaying one of the most beautiful sights the animals had ever seen.

"Oh!" gasped Shoshanna.

Tall cliffs surrounded the clearing all the way around, as if the center of the mesa had been dug and hollowed out, by a sharp garden spade, into a circular basin. Down the farthest cliff of the basin tumbled a tall and thundering waterfall, its pure, crystal clear waters collecting in a rocky pool which presumably emptied into underground springs below. Clinging to the sheer cliff walls and covering the floor of the basin were lush trees, green shrubs, vining plants, aromatic flowers.

The place was a secret paradise.

"Look! Blackberries!" said the stallion.

"And look there! I see apples on that tree!" said Ben.

"And nuts right over here!" said Casanova.

"Are those wild grapes growing against that rock?" asked Shoshanna.

"I don't know, and I don't care, 'cause I'm going for a swim and having a long, long, long, long drink!" shouted Casanova joyfully.

He plunged chest high into the delicious water. The rabbit and shrew drifted off his back and began paddling around happily. The three friends gulped water and swam and splashed and frolicked in the waterfall pool until they were fully exhausted; it was a wonder that none of them drowned from all the gulping and happy excitement. Then they gorged themselves on tender herbs and leaves, ripe fruits and nuts. Finally, they lay in the cool grass under the shade of the trees and drifted off to sleep. At first, Shoshanna and Ben slept with one eye open, staying on the alert for predators, but as there was no scent of any predator in the vicinity, they eventually let themselves fall into a very deep sleep.

The three slept for hours and hours. When they awoke, they were gazing up at a million stars twinkling in an indigo sky.

Over the next three days, the animals explored the entire basin within the mesa, which turned out to be a heavenly place indeed. Only small mammals, lizards and insects dwelled there. There were no large predators at all. There was more than enough food and water for everyone. And while the mesa animals didn't speak the same language as the three visitors, the natives were friendly to a fault, honoring Casanova, Ben and Shoshanna with gifts of their provisions, treating the three like visiting dignitaries.

Ben was the one who named the place "the mesa basin," and he was quite proud of the name. He had been pondering his formal report for the squirrels back home; he believed "the mesa basin" had both the ring of scientific credibility and the aesthetic rhyme and meter which ought to make it equally acceptable to both squirrel factions. If both faction leaders could find sufficient grounds to admit the description of the place as accurate eyewitness evidence, then they could still retain their popularity, and thus their power, within their respective factions. And this would make it easier for Ben, Shoshanna and Casanova to tell their story and avoid friction with the other animals of the forest and the meadow.

It is indeed a tragedy, Ben thought for the hundredth time, *that political polarization so often makes it impossible to readily share the bare, unvarnished truth.*

It wasn't lost on Shoshanna or Casanova, either, that their every utterance would be entered verbatim into the squirrels' official historical documents. The gravity of the responsibility to relate their story as factually as possible began to weigh on them all, so much so that the three friends spent several hours rehearsing and sussing out the optimal precise language.

"Let's not ever call the Seven a 'snake,'" said Ben, "or else some of the more contentious squirrels will latch onto the idea that we were all spooked by some common, garden variety snake, or just a rattler. They'll say that we imagined the part about the seven heads because we were all so terrified."

"We shall call the Seven exactly what it is, and give its full description," said Shoshanna firmly. "It is a gigantic red serpent, with seven heads springing from one body, and as long in body as the farmer's barn twice over, and with heads lifted up as high as that barn's loft, and as big around the middle as two of the farmer's fattest cows. And if some of those squirrels choose not to believe us, well, that's on *them*. As for me, I've already decided. I will tell the accurate truth, no matter how unbelievable it sounds, and I'll even swear before the Maker and everyone else that I *am* telling the truth, if it comes down to it."

Casanova nodded. "I'm pretty sure they're gonna want to swear us in. It'll probably be some kind of formal hearing, knowing those guys, and knowing how long they've all been arguing over the Badlands and the Worselands. But you do realize, it's not just the Seven that's going to be hard to describe. The whole story really is unbelievable, from beginning to end. Think about how we saw the two rocky pillar shapes and knew to walk toward them. And the strange way that we noticed the cleft in the rock. Then we knew to go to the right, toward this mesa basin, out in the middle of the Worselands of Worseness. And how do you even describe the Worselands of Worseness without sounding completely nuts? That place is so incredibly awful that I find it hard to believe myself! Now that we're enjoying this wonderful mesa basin, I can hardly picture that black and fiery place. But I *know* that it's out there. It *is* real." He shook his head. "I wouldn't blame those squirrels if they all thought we had gone crazy. And you know what? Not too long ago, I likely would have joined them. I would have thought you two were making it all up. But here's what I'm hoping. I'm hoping that everybody back home really *knows* you two. I'm hoping they *know* that you two don't lie or tell tall tales. I realize they don't know me very well, but you two, they already know."

Shoshanna frowned. "You're right when you say that we don't lie. Or, I should say, we *try* never to lie. We have good reputations. But, sadly, good reputations aren't always enough to withstand the damage that a persistent slanderer can cause."

Ben's expression began to mirror Shoshanna's frown. "This could get dangerous," he said quietly. "For all of us. Whenever you tell a true story that folks don't want to believe, well... let's just say that I've seen things get pretty nasty between some of the folks who inhabit that pretty little meadow of ours."

Shoshanna nodded pensively. She was thinking about a young fawn who had once seen a red wolf passing through the forest not far from the farmer's house (red wolves had been hitherto unheard of in those parts). This little fawn had duly reported this sighting to her elders. No one had believed the fawn, and she had been shunned by the entire herd for "tale bearing." It wasn't until an old buck happened to spot the wolf on his own that the fawn was reluctantly accepted back into their society. In the meantime, the fawn had been forced to survive on her own, squaring off against the many dangers that any young animal would face without the protection of her mother or the larger herd. It had been a shameful thing to do, to temporarily orphan that fawn, but it had happened. And it had happened right there in that "respectable" meadow, among "respectable" folks.

The three friends spent another two days in the mesa basin, just recuperating. They also spent those days preparing for the strenuous journey back through the Worselands of Worseness.

For all three did believe that it was time to head back; they had explored far enough. They had completed their mission to verify that the Worselands of Worseness was indeed a real place.

The discovery of the hidden paradise of the mesa basin was, in their minds, icing on the cake. And none of the three animals thought it was the Maker's will to press onward into yet more unknown territory. They were all in one accord, believing it best to return forthwith to report their findings to the squirrels.

Ben's ingenuity was indispensable in regard to the practical preparations for the homeward journey. He had spent many hours discussing human tools and construction techniques with the wisest of the squirrels back home. Ben had actually taught himself the rudiments of basket weaving—a technique which the squirrels had reverse-engineered by studying the structure of an old wicker basket which one of the farmer's daughters had abandoned in the meadow. (In fact, this was how the squirrels had learned to construct Judge Grunfeld's amazing tree lift.)

Using his teeth, Ben cut down lots of tall reeds beside the waterfall pool. He and Shoshanna wove them into pouches which could be hung on either side of the stallion's body. The work was long and laborious, but the animals adeptly applied paws and teeth to get the job done. The intent was to fill these baskets with as much fruit from the mesa basin as they could hold.

Casanova was mightily impressed as he watched the baskets finally coming together.

"Oh! I get it!" he neighed excitedly, stamping his right forehoof. "I've seen those things before! You're making those baggy things that hang off the sides of the enslaved horses who have to carry men around on their backs. I always knew those baggy things carried food, 'cause I could always smell it."

"Let's try this pair on now and see how well they fit," suggested Ben. He had just finished tying one pouch to another by two strong straps made of braided reeds.

Casanova got down on his knees. Ben grasped one of the two bags in his mouth and took a high flying leap, easily clearing the horse's back with almost a foot to spare.

"Oh, bravo, Ben," gushed Shoshanna in genuine admiration. "That was a *fine* jump!"

"Thank you," said Ben, humbly lowering his eyes to receive the compliment.

The two long straps now lay over Casanova's back, with one woven pouch resting on the ground on the port side of the horse, the other pouch on the starboard. Casanova rose clumsily from his knees to stand up straight. He twisted his neck this way and that, trying to get a look at both of his flanks.

"Yep. It worked," he harrumphed happily. "One bag hangs right there on my left side, and the other on my right. This is going to work out perfectly!"

Ben and Shoshanna went on to construct three other sets of bags, following the same pattern as the first set. When they were done, they had a total of eight pouches in which to store their precious provisions.

"I have a thought," said Shoshanna, tapping her chin with her forepaw. "Those round, hard, brown balls, covered in fuzzy hair, that have the sweet white milky stuff in them—" she paused, frowning, searching for the name.

"Ko-ko nuts," said Ben helpfully. "The birds here call them ko-ko-nuts."

"Yes," she said. "Ko-ko nuts. The birds poke holes in them, so that white fluid comes out. You've seen them do it. Do you think we could find some empty ones, and fill them up with water? I would love to be able to carry water with us. We have a long way to go, through a lot of bad country."

"Shoshanna, you are a *genius*," said Ben, and now it was time for Shoshanna to lower her eyes as she murmured her thanks.

There had to be a hundred empty shells left strewn around by the birds, but it still took the three animals a long time to find an empty coconut shell with a hole large enough to let any water flow inside. Ben finally gave up looking for the perfect shell with the perfect sized hole, and started gnawing at any available shell to make its hole large enough. Shoshanna joined him in the chewing effort. It was hard work, but, in the end, they managed to modify eight shells and fill them with water.

"We'll have to set those ko-ko nut shells very carefully inside the baskets," said Shoshanna. "If they roll around or tilt too much, all of our water will spill right back out."

"Yes," said Ben. "Well, let's hope they don't roll too much. We can pack leaves and sticks around them tightly, like a snug nest. Maybe that will help."

"Okay," she said, but her expression betrayed her fear that the plan wouldn't work.

Casanova put everyone at ease. "We know how far it is to get home, and we know that we were able to make it all the way here without any water or food at all. And the fruit we will be carrying will also have some water in it. Plus, this time, I won't be running us ragged all over the Badlands looking for that awful serpent's pretend oasis, like the fool that I was. I say, let's not worry too much about the ko-ko nuts."

Ben and Shoshanna both sighed in relief. Smiles stole back over their features.

"Good for you, Casanova," said Ben. "Spoken like the truly brave stallion that you are. Thank you. We *both* needed to hear that."

Casanova tossed his mane just a little, but then immediately bowed his head low. And this little motion proved just how much the stallion had changed, way deep down in his heart. Had he heard that same compliment a week prior, his head would have grown so big that he wouldn't have been able to get back through the narrow passage and out of the mesa. Now that Casanova was showing *real* bravery—and not just acting like a big show-off— he was *really* being praised by *real* friends who knew and loved him, warts and all. And that, my friends, is a fine feeling.

"Funny," said Shoshanna. "Casanova, just when you said 'let's not worry too much,' an old saying just popped right into my head. You know the one: 'Just keep doing your best, and pray that it's blessed, and he'll take care of the rest.'"

"Hear, hear," said Ben, nodding.

Very early the following morning, after a delightful night's sleep, the shrew and the rabbit loaded the provisions carefully into the "saddlebags" which straddled Casanova's back, while he knelt patiently. Ben had the great idea to tie all the bag straps together and to loop one of the ties around the horse's neck, like a sort of harness system. After loading the bags, Ben and Shoshanna climbed up on the horse's back and discovered that the harness also provided them with many convenient footholds to help them stay safely mounted. When Casanova carefully rose to his full height, all the bags hung perfectly and neatly in rows, and nothing slipped off his body. It was an excellent invention.

"Oooh! Wow!" said Casanova as he took his first trotting steps and felt the bags rhythmically slapping at his sides. "My, my, my, my. Ooooooh. *That* sensation will take some getting used to, I fear. I really don't know how the enslaved horses do it, day in and day out, all that stuff slapping against their flanks, and the humans on their backs hollering, 'Yah! Giddyup!'"

"Oh, I expect they get used to it. Enslaved animals get used to all sorts of things," said Shoshanna somberly.

All three fell silent for a moment as they considered the plight of their domesticated brothers and sisters.

"Are we ready?" asked Casanova, finally breaking the spell.

"Ready," said the two on his back.

I won't bore you with all the details of the return journey, because nothing exciting happened. The three friends passed through the narrow passage out of the mesa basin. They crossed the fiery, blackened Worselands of Worseness. They sniffed out their old trail and easily found their way back through the cave and out to the cleft in the rock on the other side.

When they got to the cleft, they grew very cautious and hung back inside the cave, for they were concerned that the serpent might be waiting outside for them. But no one was there. Even when they had gone a ways into the Badlands of Badness and looked back over their shoulders at the standing rock pillars, there was no silhouette of the Seven between them.

The animals discussed the possible reasons for the serpent's absence and lit on several plausible explanations, but Shoshanna's hypothesis was thought the most accurate. She believed that the Seven's entire purpose was to keep them from obeying the Master, or perhaps even to prevent them from discovering the mesa paradise, if the Seven was aware of its existence. Once they had found the mesa and had clearly conquered that obstacle, the Seven wouldn't bother to expend more of his energy on it. Their obedience had already yielded fruit; the mesa was now something they *knew* was real, by their own experience, and there would be no dissuading them or scaring them from that fact again.

"Although, I'll bet we *will* see the Seven sometime in the future. Maybe in another place. Perhaps even in a different form," she said. "In a way, I think he's always been out there, always challenging us in some way or another." She said this with a hazy expression, as though she was at that very moment watching their terrible adversary with her mind's eye, seeing some vision of him opposing them in the future.

Ben shuddered at the thought.

But Shoshanna laid a firm paw on Ben's shoulder. "Don't be afraid, Ben. His attacks will always come, but we can always win. Those attacks are just part of a bigger plan to make us braver, wiser and stronger," she said calmly. "Every time the Maker saves us from an attack, we always learn to trust him more."

Ben breathed deeply and nodded.

The journey home seemed to take only half as long as the outward leg. The way home lasted just as many grueling hours as it had the way out, but it felt to the three like the way home zipped by in no time at all! The reason may have been the fruit and water which the friends enjoyed along the way, or the easy conversation among them, or the fact that they were no longer facing unknown dangers. In fact, they had already faced the dangers of the blazing sun, the cactus spikes, the scorpions, and even the Seven himself. And they had prevailed!

Thus, it was in a merry state of triumph that they finally arrived at the edge of their familiar meadow in its lovely valley.

"Oh, bless it, bless it, *bless it!*" sighed Shoshanna, her whiskers quivering with emotion. "Our own dear meadow! *Home, sweet home!*"

The first to catch sight of the three were a litter of juvenile field mice, who squeaked excitedly and ran off in all directions, shouting at the top of their little lungs, "They're back! They're back! They're back!"

A great crowd immediately formed in the wake of the three, growing larger in number as they headed for the great squirrel tree at the far end of the meadow. Hedgehogs and opossums, rabbits and deer, mice and chipmunks, and hundreds of birds formed a chattering, dancing train of agitated admirers.

News spread quickly, probably due to the birds who flew ahead of them. When the three friends and their trailing assembly arrived at the base of the squirrel tree, they saw that Judge Grunfeld had already been lowered down, ensconced in his marvelous contraption.

The squirrel court bailiff immediately called out the traditional question to formally open the proceedings: "Who seeks the wisdom of Judge Grunfeld?"

Everyone present knew the answer to this question, of course, but anticipation was plainly evident among those assembled as they listened keenly for the response.

"We three seek the wisdom of Judge Grunfeld," said Ben, answering with the traditional reply. "That is, Mr. Casanova, Ms. Shoshanna, and myself—Benjamin, son of the rabbits of the meadow."

The entire assembly stood in complete silence, eyes fixed on Judge Grunfeld.

Grunfeld nodded once at the bailiff, who announced in his clear tenor voice, "The gallery may be seated."

Everyone in the gallery sat. Casanova knelt just long enough to allow Ben and Shoshanna to safely dismount, but quickly rose to his feet again, out of respect for the court. Ben and Shoshanna took their stand on either side of him.

Ben looked around. It seemed to him that every inhabitant of the forest and meadow was present. There had to be several thousand animals seated there, filling a huge semicircular area before the squirrel tree. All the nearby tree limbs of the forest were covered in the bright plumage of hundreds of birds, who had ceased their usually omnipresent birdsong. The silence which now hung over the forest and meadow felt eerie.

Grunfeld cleared his throat. "A formal hearing is now in session. Mr. Benjamin, please state the reason that you three have approached our venerable bench on this fine day." His bright eyes glinted, and Ben suddenly realized that even old Grunfeld had caught the contagion of excitement over the return of the three explorers.

Ben said, "If it pleases the court, we three intend to report our findings on the Badlands of Badness, and what lies beyond."

Murmurs and whispers whooshed through the assembly, but quickly died out at Grunfeld's warning glare.

"And, Your Honor," added Ben quickly, "may I request that all three of us be allowed to speak for ourselves as witnesses? Each of us waives his or her right to an advocate and agrees to be questioned by anyone you choose to appoint, in the interest of saving the court valuable time and effort, and in the interest of full transparency which will allow for the unhindered discovery of any statements of probative value."

Grunfeld's face lit up with delight. This suggestion would make his job at least a hundred times easier. "Your request is granted. This hearing shall be therefore structured in two sessions. The first session shall permit Mr. Benjamin, Mr. Casanova, and Ms. Shoshanna to relate, in uninterrupted, free narrative format, their testimonies. The second session will adhere to our usual rules of procedure for questioning a witness on the stand. During that second session, I will allow one representative of each

faction to question any, or all, of the three witnesses. Equal time
will be granted to each representative. Each faction leader may
either appoint someone else to ask questions on his behalf, or
may ask the questions himself. I want you all to remember that
this hearing is purely a fact-finding mission, and as such, my role
in it will be merely to moderate the hearing, in order to ensure
that standard rules of procedure are followed. Please be advised
that I therefore won't be rendering any finding or judgment at the
close of this hearing."

The judge paused to look pointedly at Smedley (leader of the
Possibilities Faction), and then at Barker (leader of the Empirical
Truth Faction).

"Are we clear on the rules?" Grunfeld intoned with great
authority.

Both squirrels glanced quickly at their surrounding
compadres, then nodded solemnly at Grunfeld.

Grunfeld turned to the court reporter. "Let the record
indicate that Smedley of the Possibilities Faction and Barker of
the Empirical Truth Faction have given their assent to the rules of
this hearing by nodding their heads in the presence of the entire
assembly."

The judge turned his attention to Casanova, Ben and
Shoshanna. Small flames of kindness and admiration flickered
in his eyes. "Now, let's get to what we've all been waiting for.
The testimony of our three courageous adventurers!"

The three were sworn in, and they began to tell their story
in turns, leaving out no detail—even the embarrassing ones
describing the times they felt much fear, or when they were tricked
to follow after mirages in the desert, or when they disputed with
each other about what they believed the Maker was telling them
to do next.

Whenever the three mentioned the Maker, Ben saw that many
squirrels of the Empirical Truth Faction displayed body language
that betrayed great resistance or disbelief. There were some in
that faction, though, who began leaning forward with their eyes

opened wide. Ben noticed that a surprisingly large number in the Possibilities Faction were also showing resistance to any mention of the Maker. This surprised Ben. The Possibilities members were usually willing to believe in all kinds of strange things. He knew of one such faction member who only buried his nuts and grains when the moon was full, all because a crow had once told him there could possibly be a curse on anyone who didn't.

The evident disbelief among most of the gallery was bad enough when the three described the horrific serpent known as the Seven, but it grew yet more entrenched when they described the Worselands of Worseness. The audience actually erupted in loud commentary. Grunfeld had to shout down the crowds on both sides to restore order in his court.

The description about the delightful mesa basin was more readily received, but still, Ben saw plenty of tight lipped faces and arms folded across chests among most of the squirrels.

Seeing this, Ben glanced helplessly at Shoshanna and Casanova before making his concluding statement.

"We realize that what we have described is both outlandish and astonishing," said Ben. "We ourselves feel the same way, and we were actually there to witness it! It really does sound crazy. We get that. But I assure all of you present that not one of us is exaggerating. *We saw what we saw*, and we are reporting the truth. In our descriptions today, we have neither added to, nor taken away from, the literal truth of what we all saw with our own eyes and experienced with our own bodies. If any of you would like to confirm it for yourselves, all you have to do is go out there and see it for yourselves. And before you accuse the three of us of not telling you the naked truth, I would ask you to consider this: when have any of you ever known Shoshanna or myself to tell lies, or even to exaggerate? I ask you, have we *ever* done that, in any of your recollection? And if you don't know us personally, then ask your friends who do know us very well. We have lived here among you in this meadow, all our lives. We have lived peaceably and have broken no laws. We have been true to our words and kind to our neighbors. Wouldn't you agree that it would be very out of character for Shoshanna and I to have suddenly changed into liars, and at that, so drastically? And what would we have to gain from doing so?"

A murmur went up from the assembly, and the squirrel named Barker shouted, "Objection, Your Honor! The witness is no longer testifying. He is questioning the objectivity, and therefore the honor, of this court!"

Grunfeld restored order and sighed heavily. "*Overruled*, Barker. And let it be known that there will be *no further objections* during this session. Please remember that this session allows for free narrative. Therefore, the witnesses are allowed much more latitude than usual. Hold all your objections for the second session, please, during the formal questioning. You'll have your moment to object then."

The judge turned back to the three friends. "Is there anything more you would like to share before this assembly?"

Casanova cleared his throat. "I... I have something to say. I just would like to say that... that something wonderful happened to me out there in the Badlands. You all don't know me very well, but I can testify that I was a very different horse when I first arrived in this meadow. The journey changed me a lot. For what it's worth, all my life, I was never really sure the Maker was real. I had *hoped* he was real, I suppose, and maybe in the back of my mind I guessed he was... but I didn't know for sure. And now I *know*. He *is* real. And that's... well, that's all I have to say."

Squirrels from both factions stared at the stallion with gaping mouths. Some of their faces were shocked, some disbelieving, and some angry. But a few were shining with new hope and joy.

Grunfeld glanced out at the sun, now hanging low and huge and orange just above the trees at the far end of the meadow. "This seems a good place to break for the day. Let's adjourn. We'll begin session two tomorrow at daybreak."

All the birds in the trees took off at once, making it seem

like autumn had come early as their bright forms sprinkled out like so many colorful leaves from amid the green foliage. The judge was hauled back to his high nest. The squirrel security detail immediately formed a line between the members of the two factions, likely as a precaution. The guards stood back to back, half facing the Possibilities, half facing the Empiricals. They spoke in friendly tones, but their eyes were stern and their muscles were taut. "All right, folks. All right. Let's move along now. Time to go home. Let's go. Nothing left to see here."

Thousands of the meadow animals dispersed to their various nests, holes, tunnels and burrows, chattering excitedly about all the juicy news they had just learned about the Seven, the Worselands, and the mesa basin. But about fifty of them stayed behind, surrounding Casanova, Ben and Shoshanna to thank them for their bravery. Many shook their paws or hugged them.

"I'm a believer in the Maker, just like you," said a mole to Shoshanna. "I can hardly see a thing with these eyes of mine, but he shows me visions all the time in my mind, so that I know what to do next and where to go."

"Fantastic job carrying those folks safely there and back," said a wild ram to Casanova. "You are *top notch*, in my book. Congratulations on your discovery, and I hope they do name you an official explorer in their history books, like they promised they would. You deserve it!"

A group of three small, timid squirrels approached Ben. "Sir?"

"Yes?" Ben asked, looking all around and finally seeing them in the dusky light.

"We just wanted to thank you for being so brave to tell the truth," said one.

"Oh," said Ben, taken aback. "Oh. Well, thank you. I don't suppose I really had a choice, though. You have to tell the truth, especially when you're sworn in like I was."

The second squirrel in the group piped up. "I'm not so sure about that. I think lots of people choose not to tell the whole truth, even when they are sworn in. I should know, because I hide the truth a lot. I believe in the Maker, you see. But I haven't felt safe enough to tell the rest of the squirrels that I believe in him."

The third young squirrel nodded. "If you talk about the Maker, then everyone automatically thinks you're crazy."

"Well, I could see how that would be a problem in the Empirical Faction," said Ben. "But what about the Possibilities Faction? Have you tried talking with them?"

"I did. And you saw for yourself how most of them feel about the Maker.   Everything seems to be "possible" for them, *except* for the existence of a Maker. I don't know why," said the third squirrel, shaking his head sadly.

Shoshanna was listening to this conversation. "I think I know why," she said. "Because those squirrels can sense that, once you start to really believe, you get changed. A lot. And they don't want that. They would much rather stay in control."

"You said it just right," said the first squirrel. "That's why the three of us don't belong to any faction. We don't care about power or control, one way or the other. So we don't fit anywhere at all." When he said this, a sadness flitted across his face. That single expression seemed to tell in a heartbeat the entire story of his lifetime of painful losses—his home, his family, and his former friends. The second squirrel patted his shoulder.

"Well, you will always fit with us!" said Ben. "Right, Casanova?"

"Right!" said Casanova. "Welcome to our family. You with us, Shoshanna?"

"Of course!" she said. "Anyone who loves the Maker is our family." She frowned. "Hey. That squirrel security team is heading directly our way. Wonder what they want."

The team marched briskly toward them. "All right, folks, let's break it up," said the captain.

"Break what up?" said Ben, laughing lightly. He thought the guy had to be joking.

"Let's go, let's go, time to go home," said the squirrel with a deadpan expression, this time more forcefully.

The fifty or so small animals blinked at the squirrels with huge, confused eyes, glanced at each other questioningly, then turned abruptly and headed off in all directions. Casanova, Ben and Shoshanna held their ground, though. After all they had been through, a security team wasn't likely to move them that easily.

"All right, boys, that's it for tonight," said the captain squirrel to his team. "Go home and rest up. Tomorrow's gonna be a handful, I'll warrant."

"Yes, sir," they barked.

The squirrel team departed, but their captain remained.

"I didn't want to say this in front of the others," muttered the captain in a low voice, "but I overheard the leaders of both factions talking some bad stuff just now about you three. They saw the looks on the faces of many of the meadow folk. Your story had really captured them. They also noticed that some of their own ranks were starting to believe your story." He chuckled. "And I'm one of them, but leadership doesn't know that. I've seen the Badlands myself, so I can corroborate every detail you described. Never got as far as the Worselands, but I do know how to read a face. I've done my share of interrogations, so I know a liar when I see one. You three ain't lying, and that's a fact. I believe every word of what you said. But, see, these faction leaders, they won't let their followers go that easy. They see you three as a threat to their power, know what I mean? They didn't even like the way those fifty or so animals crowded around you just now."

"Ah," said Ben, nodding.

"So... is that why your team came out this way to send everyone home? To protect us?" asked Shoshanna.

"Yep. Well, actually, to protect *all* of the folks who were standing around you. We've also got some militant faction extremists who probably would've ventured out here to attack you innocent folks. They'd have seen it as an opportunity to prove their mettle to top leadership, hoping to climb the ranks.

Open violence against you folks this evening was definitely on our radar; we've been picking up some chatter."

"Wow," said Casanova. "Well, thanks for coming out to protect us. But those squirrels couldn't have hurt me all that much, I don't suppose. And I'd have put up a good fight to protect my two best friends here."

"Oh, you'd be very surprised what a trained team of attack squirrels can do to a horse, if you can get enough of 'em working at the same time on the lower tendons," said the captain. "I've seen 'em hobble a horse good. But that's not my point. My point is how badly they would hurt the *small* animals, as a punishment for befriending you. Field mice, voles and such. Squirrels can kill those animals easy. And then you'd feel like you had *that* on your conscience. They'd hold some *real* power over you, and over the whole meadow. That level of terrorism can quash any future open-air, free-speech gatherings. Leadership knows that."

"You're right! I would feel terrible if that had happened!" said Casanova in great shock. "You mean, they'd really kill innocent animals like that, just for hanging around with us?"

"Those particular squirrels will do *anything and everything* to retain their power," said the captain. "There's no method too low or too dirty for them. Right now, as we speak, they're putting together lists of questions to bring all sorts of slander against you at tomorrow's hearing. Even after the hearing, they're never gonna stop. I know these guys. They'll be talking up all your neighbors and relatives, spreading even more false rumors about you, saying horrible things. *Anything* to take you down a notch. That's their M.O."

"Ben and I half expected as much," sighed Shoshanna. "Sadly, this isn't the first time we've seen something like this happen in our meadow. I don't suppose there is any way we could get out of the hearing tomorrow?"

"Nope. Once the judge informed the assembly that you'd be returning for the second session, and once you heard his words, that's got the same force as a subpoena," said the captain. He spread his forepaws helplessly, palms up. "And now, I'm bound to enforce it. So I do hope you three will show up voluntarily. It would make my job easier, and my day a lot nicer." He let out a shaky laugh.

"We are law-abiding animals," said Ben quickly. "We'll all be there. And so *what* if a few ornery squirrels ask us a bunch of ridiculous questions? We'll just answer them the best we can, and then we'll go home."

The captain frowned. "I hope that's all it comes to. I hope it ends well for you." He sighed. "Good night, folks. Make sure you three travel together tonight until you each get safely back to your homes. And even then, maybe keep one eye open while you sleep."

He glanced this way and that, then darted off in the direction of the great squirrel tree.

Ben, Shoshanna and Casanova pondered his last words in shocked silence.

"Ben, would you mind if I stayed with you tonight?" asked Shoshanna.

"Oh, please do," he said. "That would put my mind more at ease, just to know that you are safe and sound."

Shoshanna threw back her head and laughed. "I only asked to stay with you because I wanted to be sure that *you* were protected!"

A goofy smile of embarrassed realization spread over Ben's face as he saw that she was right. Shoshanna was easily the fiercer fighter of the two of them. As powerfully as a rabbit can defend itself with its strong hind legs and razor sharp claws, anyone would rather face a rabbit than a shrew in full-on attack mode.

Casanova nudged Ben's neck gently with his nose. "Come on. Let's all head back to your burrow. I'll spend the night just outside your tunnel. That way, Shoshanna can protect me, too."

All three burst into laughter.

Early the next morning, the three explorers found themselves standing before Judge Grunfeld at the great squirrel tree, being sworn in again. The crowd had somehow grown even larger than the day before. Word must have spread that session two would be packed with drama, as Barker and Smedley were each scheduled to conduct formal questioning of the witnesses.

The day went every bit as dreadfully as the squirrel captain had suggested it would. Ben, Shoshanna and Casanova were pummeled mercilessly, from both sides, by questions which implied they had stretched the truth, or were mentally ill, or were morally deficient, or all of the above. Sometimes, the questions positioned the three witnesses as mere pawns in an attack of the opposing faction's core beliefs; other times, the questions attacked the individual witnesses themselves. But the single common denominator of all the questions was "relentless attack."

To their credit, Casanova, Shoshanna and Ben kept their tempers and answered truthfully, the best they could. But one particular exchange, at the end of the eighth hour of questioning, finally reduced Shoshanna to tears. This happened to occur during Barker's inquiries, although Smedley had been no less aggressive toward her throughout the day.

"So, Ms. Shoshanna," said Barker as he strutted back and forth, chest puffed out, before the members of his faction, the Empirical Truthers. "Let's return one more time to your description of this so-called 'Seven.'"

Here, Barker turned away from Shoshanna, faced his faction, lifted his eyebrows slightly, and gave a little grin that appeared to let them in on a secret joke. His expression seemed to say, *Let's humor this poor shrew, shall we? She clearly can't be in her right mind, poor dear.*

Barker turned back again to face the shrew. "Now, at one point in your testimony, you used the plural pronoun *'they.'*" He consulted a strip of soft, smooth bark which was covered in writing. "Ah. Here it is. You said, and I quote, '*They* were telling us that the Badlands were actually a good land,' unquote. But elsewhere in your testimony, you referred repeatedly to the Seven as *'he.'"* Barker chuckled lightly. "Well, which is it, Ms. Shoshanna? Were there more than one snake present, or was it just the one? Perhaps, in the stress of the moment, you didn't remember clearly what you saw. Is that a *possibility*?" Here, Barker stressed the word "possibility" and fired a sharp smirk in the direction of the Possibility faction, who seethed at him.

"Well," said Shoshanna, twisting her forepaws in her lap, "it's... it's a bit hard to explain. The serpent definitely seemed to me as though it had one, single mind, or at least unified thoughts, yet the heads were capable of moving independently, which gave the impression of separate entities. However, whenever the thing spoke, all the heads spoke in complete unison. It was a very eerie thing to experience."

"Oh, yes, I imagine so, I imagine so," soothed Barker, nodding his head in a show of compassion. "What a terrible fright it must have caused you."

"Objection, Your Honor. Counsel is testifying," said Smedley, rising to his feet.

"Sustained," grumbled Grunfeld. "Ask a question, Mr. Barker. Let's get on with it."

"I'll move on, Your Honor," said Barker amiably. "Ms. Shoshanna, you stated several times during your testimony yesterday that you, quote, 'heard the Maker.' Now, this so-called voice you purport to be able to hear; would you describe it as some kind of *audible* voice?"

Shoshanna looked out at the crowd, then back at Barker. She understood that his intention was to make her appear to be crazy, but she answered firmly, with a level tone. "No, Mr. Barker. It is not a voice that I hear with my physical ears. It is an understanding that I get within my heart."

"Ah. 'An understanding that you get within your heart.' Ah. Yes. I see," said Barker, turning to look meaningfully at the Empirical Truthers. The left side of his face turned up into a half grin, and several members of his faction chuckled aloud.

"Objection!" shouted Smedley.

Grunfeld, clearly exhausted by the entire day's worth of shenanigans and political posturings, sighed and groaned. "Don't make me clear the gallery; let's have order, please. And, Mr. Barker, if you don't ask a question that actually seeks to uncover or clarify a point of fact, I will hold you in contempt. You've been walking on thin ice all day, and I've just about had it with you."

Smedley's face flickered with delight over this harsh reprimand of his adversary.

But Grunfeld caught sight of Smedley's fleeting expression. "I've about had it with *both* of you. So watch that attitude, yourself, Mr. Smedley," said Grunfeld. He turned wearily to Barker and waved a paw lamely at him. "Proceed, Mr. Barker."

Barker smiled ingratiatingly at the judge, gave a small bow of his head, then turned to Shoshanna. "Would it not be more accurate to say, Ms. Shoshanna, that you *believed* or *thought* you heard the voice of the Maker in your heart?"

It was at this point that tears sprang from Shoshanna's eyes and ran down her furry face. "How can I possibly answer that question to your satisfaction, Mr. Barker? No matter what I answer, I could never provide empirical evidence that I heard a voice. Nor could I provide empirical evidence that I merely *thought* I heard that voice."

Barker turned to the judge. "Your honor? A little help, please?"

"You must answer the question, Ms. Shoshanna," ordered Grunfeld, but gently.

"I didn't *think* that I heard the Maker," she said forcefully. "I *heard.* And the evidence that his voice is real can be found in the way our journey played out, Mr. Barker, if you'll only choose to see it as evidence. For example, I heard that we ought to go forward and not retreat. I saw the picture of the two columns of stone, heard a command, and then we headed for them. I realized, because of that same voice's warning, that the serpent was sending us after pictures of a false oasis which would be dangerous for us to chase after. Because of that same voice, I knew to turn to the right rather than the left when we traveled the Worselands of Worseness, and that's exactly how we found the mesa."

"Or, you got lucky," pointed out Barker.

"Your honor!" squealed Smedley, hopping to his feet in outrage. "He's testifying *again! And* he's badgering the witness!"

"Wrap it *up*, Mr. Barker!" shouted Grunfeld angrily.

"No more questions for this witness, Your Honor," said Barker in a congenial tone as he swiftly retreated from Grunfeld's bench.

Two hours later, the questioning of all three witnesses was finally over with. Everyone in the court and the gallery went home, leaving Casanova, Ben and Shoshanna standing alone in the dusky clearing.

"Ten hours!" moaned Ben. "Ten hours of questioning. I feel like a piece of shredded straw. And for what?"

Casanova shook his head in disbelief. "No one learned anything new about our story. No one got any real clarification of the facts. What was the point of that exercise?"

"The point," said Shoshanna, "was to wreck our reputations. And I think Barker and Smedley both managed to do quite a lot of that. And they had another reason to do what they did. It was an opportunity to show themselves strong, in public, against the opposing party. Each was able to rile up his political base against the other, and at the same time try to prevent any of their followers from believing in our story, or in the Maker. That hearing was a real win-win for them."

"And a lose-lose for us," said Ben mournfully.

"Mmmm... I don't think so," said Shoshanna. "A lot of those animals we met with last night were watching us closely today, and I was watching them right back. They remained compassionate toward us. They were *proud* of us. They knew we were telling the truth all the more, because we didn't act out in rage or offense during the questioning. I think our testimony today actually convinced *more* folks about the Maker, rather than less! I think the faction leaders' plan might have backfired just a little...at least regarding the folks who are pure in heart. Those are the real seekers of the truth, so they can see through the fog a little better than most."

"Huh," said Casanova. "Let's hope so."

Life in the meadow over the following months would show whether Shoshanna had been right about that.

As time went by, Casanova, Ben and Shoshanna were shunned or mocked by most of the folks in the meadow. The whole thing reminded Shoshanna of the fawn who saw the red wolf, as their own situation unfolded in nearly a duplicate manner. The more virulent members of the squirrel factions were relentless in the spreading of false and malicious gossip about the three friends, and they never seemed to ease up on this activity.

But another amazing thing was happening at the same time. Those who had always secretly believed in the Maker started speaking more publicly, having watched the bravery of the three witnesses at the hearing. And when they themselves started getting the same bad treatment, even more good-hearted folks came to believe that maybe what this minority espoused regarding the Maker could actually be true. Those who believed in the Maker, after all, were the only ones acting in a kind and loving manner, while everyone else was being straight-up mean to them. It made quite a contrast.

By the beginning of autumn, there were a total of seventy animals in the meadow who identified themselves as believers in the Maker. Most became close friends with Ben, Shoshanna and Casanova. But, as there were thousands of animals in that community (if you include the surrounding forest), these seventy believers represented only a tiny minority. Life was harsh and difficult for the believers without being able to count on the usual support of all the other animals in the ecosystem.

One day, a young field mouse approached Shoshanna. This little mouse was a believer, and her name was Miriam.

"Miss Shoshanna, may I speak with you in private?" asked Miriam.

They went behind a large copse, and there Miriam poured her heart out to Shoshanna. She spoke about growing tired of getting spit on, bitten, and chased away by other animals. She talked about how the unbelieving mice had purposely gathered extra food for the winter above and beyond what they would need, but wouldn't share any with her family. And this was unheard of; mice *always* share their food with other mice, no matter what. And last of all, she spoke passionately about the mesa basin.

"Oh, how I wish I could see that beautiful place!" she sighed. "I dream about it frequently. I can see it so clearly in my dreams. It feels so real to me! Oh, Miss Shoshanna, could we ever make a visit there?"

In a flash, Shoshanna knew exactly what had to be done. In fact, she could suddenly see the Maker's plan as clear as day.

"Go and gather everyone you know, everyone who believes in the Maker," she said to Miriam. "Have them meet me here behind the copse, exactly when the sun comes down to touch the tops of the far trees at the meadow's end."

Shoshanna herself rushed off to find Ben and Casanova. She found them beside the burbling creek where they had all first met.

"We're going back," she said abruptly.

"Well, hello to you, too," joked Ben good naturedly. Then he took a second look at her serious expression. "Going back? Where?"

"Back to the mesa basin."

"Huh," said Casanova thoughtfully. But his right forehoof scratched at the earth in a combination of excitement, nervousness, and joy. "Huh," he said again.

"Do you mean... all three of us?" asked Ben. "Is this... is this from the Maker?"

"Yup!" said Shoshanna, now erupting in smiles.

The joy was now infectious. Ben hopped straight up in the air and came back down on all fours. "I feel it! You are right! We're moving there! We get to live there! Forever!" His left back leg thumped repeatedly on the earth: *bump bump bump bump bump!*

"That's right!" said Shoshanna.

"Just think," said Casanova dreamily. "No more angry folks calling us names, and always trying to throw rocks at me. It's been so hard for me to behave and be good. Most days I want to give those nasty animals some what-for, but the Maker keeps telling me to forgive them and be kind to them. Over in the mesa, I will finally be able to relax a little. Let down my guard. That will be great!"

"And it's such a beautiful place to live!" sighed Ben. "Remember all the flowers, and all the fruit?"

"I've called a meeting," said Shoshanna. "Because it won't be just us three this time. It's going to be everyone who believes. All seventy of us."

"Whoa!" said Ben. "Even the old ones? And the little babies? How will we ever get them across the Badlands... never mind the Worselands?"

"I saw a picture in my mind," said Shoshanna. "Casanova and the wild rams will carry the little ones and the weak ones in baskets on their backs. The same way we carried fruit back from the mesa."

"That's brilliant," said Ben. "Well, we'd better get started now making the baskets. Winter is just around the corner!"

At the evening meeting with all the believers, Shoshanna shared Miriam's words which had prompted Shoshana's vision of all of them moving to the mesa. Everyone present was instantly in joyful agreement; they all agreed to assist in making the baskets and gathering provisions for the hard journey ahead. Everyone was sick of living life in the meadow; they were fully ready to take the seemingly riskier path that the Maker had indicated. Frankly, a journey through the Worselands with friends who loved them seemed better than staying in a lush meadow among folks who hated them.

Over the next week, they all worked hard at their preparations for the journey. Though they tried at first to work in secret, word quickly spread throughout the meadow. It is very difficult to disguise the movements of seventy animals, all cutting down reeds by the creek, weaving them into strange shapes, and gathering up more food than usual. Especially when gossipy birds can fly overhead and chat up all the neighbors about your business.

As the baskets were being completed, unbelievers often stopped by to watch and to mock the effort.

"What're you doing? Making it easier for the farmer to haul your carcasses off to market once you die out there?" called one.

"Those baskets look about as strong as a spider's web!" chortled another. "Good luck with that!"

But the believers never looked up from their work.

That wonderful morning finally arrived when they were ready to embark. Just before they did, Miriam came up to Shoshanna.

"I had another dream last night," she said. "I think it means something."

"Go on," said Shoshanna, leaning forward with great interest.

"I dreamed we were standing in front of the Seven. We weren't even running away. We just stood there, very calm. And, oh, the Seven, he was very big and scary, just as you described at the hearing. Anyhow, in the dream, we had seven stones and we threw one at each head of the serpent. On each stone was a different word: Maker-Presence, Wisdom, Understanding, Counsel, Strength, Knowledge, and Maker-Fear."

"Huh," said Shoshanna. "You're right about that dream being important. I *must* remember those seven words. Will you help me learn them by heart?"

Together, the two recited them over and over.

"But I'm not sure what those words are supposed to mean, Miss Shoshanna," said Miriam.

"Me either. Some of them I believe I *might* understand, but others I don't," admitted Shoshanna.

Shoshanna found Ben and Casanova, who were already helping load the frail ones and the little ones into their baskets.

"I just learned something very important from Miriam," said Shoshanna.

She told them the dream about the seven stones and the seven words.

"That is *very* important," said Ben. "You're right."

"How do you know?" asked Casanova.

"I just know, deep inside. We have to learn those words by heart, and also learn what they mean," said Ben.

"That is the exact same thing that I said," said Shoshanna excitedly.

"I have an idea. Why don't we ask *everyone* to learn the words? The more people that know them by heart, the less chance we will forget," suggested Casanova.

"Brilliant!" said Ben.

The three called out to the rest of the seventy animals. "Everyone! Just stop work for a moment. We have something to tell you."

The three told everyone the little mouse's dream.

"We think this dream is very important," said Casanova. "We want everyone to learn the seven words by heart. And we all need to ask the Maker to show us what these words really mean. Okay?"

"Okay!" said all the animals, great and small.

They returned to their preparations, reciting the seven words back and forth to each other as they worked. Within a half hour, everyone was ready to go, and nearly everyone knew all seven words by heart.

The group embarked. They made their way slowly and carefully through the meadow. Strapped to the back of Casanova were eight baskets, some carrying small animals, others carrying grains, fruits and seeds. Four wild rams also each carried two large baskets apiece, holding small animals and provisions. The rest of the party followed on foot as they were able. It was a rag-tag group, certainly. But the strong scent of the Maker's full blessing was hanging in the air.

As they passed out of the meadow and into the forest, the seventy could hear the last of the mocking taunts of their former neighbors.

"Good riddance! Hope you all die out there," called one particularly nasty voice, its owner well hidden behind a forest tree.

"Don't listen to them," said Ben calmly to the group. "They don't know what they're saying."

But he saw fear in the eyes of all the little ones.

The journey beyond the farm and through the Badlands was just as expected. The group ran across a scorpion and a rattlesnake, but neither took any notice of the believers, as they seemed to be fully engrossed in their own business. Or perhaps they merely put on a nonchalant and nonthreatening air, recognizing that they'd better not mess with a group of seventy animals.

Casanova adeptly selected the safest and broadest path possible to avoid getting entangled in cacti, but even so, one of the moles got stuck in his side by a cactus spine, as he couldn't see where he was going very well. The whole group had to stop and help remove it.

Water quickly became an issue. There had been no easy way for the group to bring along any water, aside from the four old coconut shells that had originally come from the mesa. Those four shells were soon emptied, as the very young and the very old desperately needed that water and used it up quickly.

"It's not all that long a journey," reassured Ben in a hopeful tone. "Everyone try and keep the passengers well shaded, and we will all arrive at the beautiful mesa before you know it."

The pouches being carried by Casanova and the four rams had been designed with floppy woven lids for the express purpose of providing shade to their passengers, but even with the lids down, it was still exceptionally hot in those baskets.

Secretly, Ben began to worry, *What if someone dies along the way?*

Each time that worry arose in his heart, he cried inside himself to the Maker for help.

"Don't let anyone die, please," he prayed under his breath. "Please, please, please."

Shoshanna and Casanova spent their time pondering the seven words and what they might mean. Ben began to do this as well, and the practice of reciting the words quelled his anxiety. Occasionally, the three would speak together about the words and their meaning, but these discussions were brief and scattered. Speaking in that stifling and arid air seemed to expend far too much energy and moisture.

After what seemed like endless hours of trudging through shifting sands, Shoshanna spotted the two rocky columns in the distance.

"Hurray!" shouted all the animals. They knew that the rocky columns marked the three-quarter point in the journey to the mesa, their future home.

As they approached the columns, though, the silhouette of the gigantic serpent made itself apparent.

"This looks just like it did in my dream," said Miriam to Shoshanna, who had opted to ride beside her on Casanova's back.

"Yes," said Shoshanna. "And I'm being told that we will not need to run away this time. This time, we will pass straight between those columns, triumphantly. But how that can possibly happen, I don't yet see. It has to do with the seven words on the seven stones from your dream."

The seventy drew up within fifty yards or so of the columns. They could clearly see the Seven, and its seven heads could clearly see all of them. The serpent was just as terrifying in real life as advertised. In fact, many of the folks thought that the three witnesses' vivid descriptions of the serpent hadn't done justice to its true size and fearsome power. Several of them began to grow faint from fear.

"Ahh... I see that the foolish ones have returned," sneered the Seven. "And with many new friends in tow. Have you finally come to your senses and decided to seek my great wisdom and assistance, after all?"

A sudden boldness came over Shoshanna so that she shook with emotion. "Why should we seek wisdom and help from a counterfeit and a sham like you? For that is *exactly* what you are. You proudly call yourself the Seven, as if *you* are anything good or holy! Matter of fact, I can't even stand saying your name. Seven is the *Maker's* number, not yours, you copy-cat! You're just trying to take away his honor and glory. You want to get everyone to worship you instead of him! Well, it's not going to work!"

All seven heads snapped like a bolt of lightning in her direction. Rage flickered in their eyes. But a cool tone emanated from the mouths.

"Perhaps you might give careful consideration to my initial proposition, that you join your heart and soul to mine, little shrew. For you are feisty, and strong willed, and most courageous. I could certainly use a brave warrior like you in my vast army. Oh, and I could offer you *far* more than the Maker offers. What is it that you most desire? Fame? Fortune? Honor? Glory? What have you obtained in your short life from that Maker of yours, other than suffering and sorrow? Don't you see that he is never there for you when you most need him? Indeed, where is he when life gets difficult? Where is he right now, as you pant and thirst and face great danger? But, now, cast your eyes upon *me*. Look upon my powerful and glorious form. Here I *am*. *I am!* I am always *here* for you."

The first word from the first stone of the dream filled Shoshanna's mouth. *Maker-presence.* And even as it filled her mouth, she felt the Maker there, in her and around her and all among the seventy animals whom he so dearly loved.

"Wrong, liar," said Shoshanna calmly. "The Maker *is* present, right now. He is *always* here. And there is nowhere in the sky above or in the earth below that he is not present!"

The serpent head on the far left suddenly began to look dazed as though it had been struck by a mighty blow. The head flopped over, and the neck whipped randomly to and fro for a moment before finally lying still in the dust.

The remaining six heads of the serpent looked aghast for a split second, but quickly resumed their calm expressions and charming speech.

"But, my dear ones, while he may be *present* from time to time, can he really give you such wisdom and understanding as I have? Do you not realize that I know all the ways of this world, for I control them all? And with my wisdom comes great power over all the dark things, the secret things, the great enchanted powers of gloom that lie underneath the below, and below the underneath. Do you not wish to partake of such secret magic? Only give your hearts fully to me, and every dark secret with all of its dark power shall be yours to wield exactly as you will."

Ben spoke up this time. "We don't rely on our own wisdom or our own understanding. Everything we need to know, we learn from the Maker. We realize that his ways are different from our ways, and so we trust *him* to know best. He explains everything we need to know as we encounter each trial. And no, we don't want any power and control. We want *him* to have all the power and control."

"*Wisdom* and *understanding!* Ben just said the next two words on the stones from my dream!" whispered Miriam excitedly to Shoshanna.

"And he probably didn't even think about what he was saying, because the Maker was giving him words to say. I could tell," nodded Shoshanna. "That's what happened to me earlier."

By the time this short conversation between the shrew and the mouse had ended, two more serpent heads were lying on the ground, lifeless.

The remaining heads were now having a more difficult time concealing their nervousness.

"But, but, but, but... *wait!*" squealed the heads in a high pitched fervor. "Wait a moment," they added, this time in a lowered voice, and with a forced calm. "I can be an *excellent* guide for you through the Worselands. I have intimate knowledge of the terrain. In fact, I know of a shortcut to take you through. If you'll agree to join forces with me against the Maker, I can be your guide. You all can ride on my body, and I can carry you through. For I am strong and mighty!"

"No thanks," said Casanova. "I'd rather die than join the likes of you, and everyone here with me feels the same way. Why should we accept guidance or help from a horrible liar like you, when we have the counsel and strength of the Maker himself? He created the Badlands and he created the Worselands. He already knows all there is to know! And frankly, it really ticks me off that you even dare to compare your piddly so-called counsel, or your knowledge, or your strength, to his!" Casanova tossed his mane in righteous indignation.

Three more serpent heads, this time on the right side of the serpent, writhed and fell into the dust.

"Casanova just said *counsel, strength* and *knowledge!*" whispered the mouse.

"He sure did," said Shoshanna, who was beaming with loving pride for her equine friend.

Now, only one serpent head still remained aloft, the center one, and it was rising higher and higher. The eyes had turned red and were filling up with pure hatred and rage.

"Seeing that you all refuse to bow to me, and to show me the reverence and honor due me," bellowed the single head, "then *you shall feel my wrath!*"

The head reared back and made ready to strike, but a blinding light suddenly appeared like a flash and stood between the Seven and the seventy.

Instantly, all of the animals shook and quaked, filled with a holy terror that was somehow mixed up with adoring love. All of the animals fell to their knees or flat on their stomachs and put their faces in the desert dust.

Maker-fear, thought Shoshanna as she lay flat on her stomach on Casanova's back, eyes closed. *That's what this is.*

She had felt Maker-fear before. It was the deepest and purest kind of awe. It was far more overwhelming than any fear she had ever felt while running for her life from a predator. She had learned that she never could stand up for very long in the presence of Maker-fear. She usually collapsed to the ground.

The seventy animals, with their eyes squeezed shut against the glorious and pure light, heard, rather than saw, that unholy serpent's end. They heard the terrified screams of the serpent as it begged for mercy.

"No, please don't! Don't send me *there!* No! No! *Please! No!*"

A great wind suddenly rushed between the rocks, as strong as a tornado. It was so strong that the animals would have surely been swept away except for the staying power of that pure and holy light ahead of them. When the wind died away, the light was gone, and that evil serpent was nowhere to be found.

You might think that all the animals would have gotten up right then and cheered, but they were still shaking like leaves and lying very still.

There are holy moments in a person's life— moments when you *do not speak* and you *do not even dare to think.* It's all you can do to just experience the moment, having only the awesome realization that you might actually live to tell about it.

For the seventy, this was one of those holy moments.

After about five minutes of lying very still, the animals gradually got up and shook the dust off themselves. Some were weeping, but it was not a sad or forlorn weeping. It was a beautiful and joyful weeping. Some were smiling to themselves. But no one was speaking. Not yet.

They passed in silence between the two rock columns and headed down into the Worselands of Worseness.

And here, another amazing thing happened. The same brilliant light appeared again, but this time, it wasn't so fearsome to look at. It took the shape of a tall cloud and went ahead of them to lead the way. It wound between the flows of molten lava, choosing a perfectly safe and level path for the seventy.

Casanova, recalling his first trip through this region, was amazed to realize that he didn't even feel the scorching heat coming up from the ground where they were now walking. And the smaller animals on foot behind him didn't complain of any burning on their paw pads, either. It was as though they were all being shielded from it. Other animals in the group later reported that, immediately upon seeing the brilliant cloud, their terrible thirst had also somehow disappeared.

As soon as the cloud led them up to the entrance crack in the mesa, the cloud vanished.

Casanova swiftly led the way inside. All the animals followed, passing through the curving, twisting passage, deep into the mesa's rocky interior.

And what a view struck their eyes as they emerged from that passage and finally saw that inner basin.

There was the pure, cold waterfall and its crystal clear pool.

There were the fruit-laden trees and vines.

There was the sweet, green grass.

It was there, inside the mesa, that the celebration finally broke loose. The animals jumped and danced and laughed and sang. They chattered and splashed in the water and rolled around on the green turf. And all the native animals of the mesa—the birds, lizards, and mammals who recognized Casanova, Ben, and Shoshanna from their earlier visit—rushed over to welcome their many new friends.

And they all lived there together, happily, forever and ever and ever.

Lisa Cummins and her late husband Jim Cummins have written many books, both fiction and nonfiction. They love the Maker very much, and this love has always inspired their writing. If you would like to read more of their books, please visit their author page:

amazon.com/author/lisa-m-cummins